He Was Beautiful, Sinfully Beautiful.

"Blade, I . . . I saw the light and came up to turn it off. I never thought I'd find you here."

He smiled. "I'm glad to see you, Jenny. Come on in."

It seemed wanton, his lying there, obviously naked under the sheet, with the soft spring darkness outside. They had only to turn out the light and touch each other. . . .

"What are you doing here, Blade?" Her voice sounded strange and tight.

"This is where I used to live, remember? This is my home. I hope we can be friends."

Her mind screamed silently. How could she be friends with him? Didn't he know what just looking at him did to her . . . ?

ANN MAJOR

has developed an engrossing storywriting style that has won her many admirers. She lives in Texas with her husband and three children, and not only writes but manages a business and household as well.

Dear Reader:

SILHOUETTE DESIRE is an exciting new line of contemporary romances from Silhouette Books. During the past year, many Silhouette readers have written in telling us what other types of stories they'd like to read from Silhouette, and we've kept these comments and suggestions in mind in developing SILHOUETTE DESIRE.

DESIREs feature all of the elements you like to see in a romance, plus a more sensual, provocative story. So if you want to experience all the excitement, passion and joy of falling in love, then SILHOUETTE DESIRE is for you.

For more details write to:

Jane Nicholls
Silhouette Books
PO Box 236
Thornton Road
Croydon
Surrey CR9 3RU

ANN MAJOR
Golden Man

Silhouette Desire
Originally Published by Silhouette Books
division of
Harlequin Enterprises Ltd.

First published in Great Britain 1985 by Mills & Boon Ltd, 15–16 Brook's Mews, London W1A 1DR

© Ann Major 1985

Silhouette, Silhouette Desire and Colophon are Trade Marks of Harlequin Enterprises B.V.

ISBN 0 373 05198 0

22–0985

Made and printed in Great Britain by Richard Clay (The Chaucer Press) Ltd, Bungay, Suffolk

Other Silhouette Books by Ann Major

Silhouette Desire

Dream Come True
Meant to Be
Love Me Again
The Wrong Man

Silhouette Special Edition

Brand of Diamonds

*For further information about
Silhouette Books please write to:*

Jane Nicholls
Silhouette Books
PO Box 236
Thornton Road
Croydon
Surrey CR9 3RU

This book is dedicated to
a special man in my life,
my brother—David Major

Golden Man

1

How does dinner and a night of passion and wild, irresponsible sex sound?'' Chuck whispered in Lilly's ear with a lusty chuckle just as Jenny Zachery walked into her secretary's office.

The room was instantly, nervously hushed as Jenny flicked cool green eyes over her two employees.

Looking sheepish, Chuck removed his hand from Lilly's shoulder and stood up. Lilly suppressed a giggle and began rifling through a stack of papers on her desk, trying to look dutiful even though she felt deeply embarrassed.

Lilly admired her boss, even though Jenny Zachery was so poised that she scarcely seemed human at times and so proper that Lilly could not imagine any man daring such an impropriety with her. It was a pity, really. Not only was Jenny beautiful, but beneath the polish Lilly suspected she was a warm and vibrant woman.

"Did you have a nice lunch, Mrs. Zachery?" Lilly managed.

Jenny nodded just as Lilly, in her agitation, knocked several file folders onto the carpet. "Oh, dear. I'm sorry about that, Mrs. Zachery. I didn't mean to be so clumsy."

"I'll get them," Chuck said hastily, stooping to retrieve the spilled contents of the folders.

"I trust you two have been working while I was out," Jenny said. Lilly flushed. "Any calls, Lilly?"

"Only Mr. Kilpatrick."

"I'll return his call from my office. And Lilly—"

"Yes, ma'am?"

"Hold my calls. I'm taking the rest of the day off."

Lilly was stunned. For the first time she forgot her embarrassment over Chuck's remark and saw how pale and unusually vulnerable Jenny looked. "You're not ill, Mrs. Zachery? If there's anything I can do?"

Jenny Zachery scarcely ever took any time away from the resort. When she did it could only mean that something was terribly wrong.

"Thank you, Lilly, but I'm all right. It's just that this is the day, two years ago, that Dean—" Jenny's green eyes grew luminous. She couldn't go on, but she didn't have to.

Lilly's voice was compassionate. "Of course, Mrs. Zachery."

Everyone in the little Texas ranching community of Zachery Falls not only remembered Dean Zachery, they revered his memory. And when they had entombed the man, they had placed his widow upon a pedestal. What none of them knew was that to Jenny the pedestal sometimes seemed so dangerously high and wobbly that she feared she would slip from it. She was afraid of the weaknesses in her character that lay hidden just beneath the surface.

But then, as a preacher's daughter growing up in a small town, Jenny had learned early that wicked impulses had to be locked away, that any indiscretion would be severely punished. She'd had to pretend not to mind that she was a plain, gawky child, when in reality she had longed to be beautiful. She'd been smart, with straight-A report cards, but deep in her heart she'd envied Susan Harper, who hadn't cared about A's, who was popular with the boys, who wasn't afraid to get into trouble. Girls like Susan led exciting lives. Jenny had longed to have fun instead of being so shy and stodgily serious.

Things hadn't changed when she grew older, though her awkward looks gave way to a mature, womanly beauty. She'd remained shy, but people now thought she was poised. There were even those who mistook her for a snob when they first met her. No one suspected that buried beneath her wall of quiet reserve were surging desires that she only half understood.

Jenny was good at locking things deep inside her. Only today it was more difficult than usual. Today, when the bluebonnets were so thick that the fields seemed like waving oceans, she was poignantly reminded of other days long ago. Her memories filled her with such aching nostalgia that she felt she would burst from the pain.

Jenny envied Lilly her young man, who could lightly joke as Dean had never joked with her. Jenny wanted to have fun, to be young again, to do all the things she'd never gotten to do. She didn't want to be a respectable widow with a two-year-old daughter to raise. She fervently wished she could escape the burden of the ranch and the resort. All of it was too much.

She should marry Mike Kilpatrick and let him bail her out of her troubles. That's what everyone expected her to do. Why then couldn't she say yes to Mike, as she'd once said yes to Dean when she'd been troubled and wanted to escape her problems? She wanted so desperately to be able to lean on a man again. But hadn't she told herself she needed to stand alone? There was something wrong with marrying a man because you couldn't handle your own life.

Jenny swept from the room to her own office before her thin veneer of calm cracked. Once inside she closed the door and sank back against it. With one hand she rubbed her aching neck. Every muscle in her body felt tense.

As always, she was dressed stunningly. She was overdressed for the casual ranching community, but then she was running, or rather trying to run a first-class resort that catered to wealthy Texans from Houston, Austin, and San Antonio. Dean had taught her that it was necessary to dress the part, and her luncheon today with a Houston businessman whose firm was seeking a conference center in which to conduct summer seminars had been important. She wore a linen safari shirt, cotton skirt, and a designer "leopard" fur and rhinestone belt. Dean would have approved. Just as he would have approved of her simple gold jewelry and the sophistication of her upswept hairdo. Like her father, he had never liked her rich brown hair to cascade wildly about her shoulders. But there were other things he wouldn't have liked, had he known of them.

"Oh, Dean. Why did you leave me, when I needed you so? What am I going to do?" she murmured aloud as she thought of the overwhelming financial problems of the resort. How had things begun to go so badly? She felt so inadequately prepared to solve all the problems confronting her.

She'd married Dean right out of high school and had been too busy working while he was in college in San Marcos to go to college herself. Besides, at the time she'd wanted to concentrate on her marriage. Dean's sudden death had thrust her into the business world at a very bad time. The Texas economy as a whole had been depressed because of the oil business, and she hadn't realized that she'd need to do so much promotion for the resort. Overwhelmed by her grief, she'd let last summer slip by, and hadn't realized until it was nearly over that her bookings were down twenty-five percent from the summer before. And the summer months were the peak season. Why hadn't she taken more of an interest in the operation of the resort when Dean was alive? Too late she'd realized her mistake in letting him handle everything.

Just thinking of all this was causing her headache to grow worse. Maybe she should return Mike's call. He always made her feel better. Wearily she crossed the room and lifted the telephone receiver on her glossy pecan desk. Dean's desk. Today everything reminded her of Dean, of her loss, of how alone she was.

The secretary forwarded her call.

"Hello, Mike."

"Jenny." His voice was warm and vital. "Is the church social still on?"

"You know it is. I'm looking forward to it. I need to get out and see people. So does Cathy."

"How's she been this week?"

"Terrible."

"She's two."

"Some comfort." Jenny sighed. "She put a grandaddy

longlegs in her mouth this morning. I screamed at her and made her cry."

"I don't blame you."

"Mothers are supposed to nurture. I'm afraid I get too impatient."

"Nonsense. You're a perfect mother." His voice lowered. "In fact, I think you're absolutely perfect in every way. You looked gorgeous Saturday night."

Perfect. It was a compliment, but it grated. That's what everyone thought, that she was perfect. Virtuous, hardworking, self-sacrificing were the labels the town pinned on her. "She's such a serious little thing, the Widow Zachery. So quick to help a needy neighbor, and don't forget her church work. Such an admirable young woman. And so old-fashioned. Wish there were more like her." Jenny knew what was said behind her back. How little they knew about the real, the wicked Jenny.

Only one man knew—and he had not been her husband.

Thank heavens he'd left Zachery for good when she'd married Dean, returning only for Caleb's funeral, and then later for Dean's. How could she have borne the insolent knowledge in his eyes? Worse, how could she have borne the secret desire in her own heart?

For an instant, before she stifled the vision, the image of Blade Taylor rose in her mind's eye. The mere thought of his virile maleness evoked a treacherously wicked quiver in the pit of her stomach. She remembered the feel of lean brown arms circling her bare flesh and pulling her against his muscled torso. As if it were only yesterday she could hear the sound of the creek, smell the cedar and wild flowers, feel the texture of the soft grasses against her naked skin as he pulled her beneath him. She felt the intimacy of sensual lips claiming hers. She could taste tobacco and liquor on his breath as he explored her mouth with his tongue. Too, she remembered the scent of him, the smell of leather and horses that clung to him from the long ride they had taken to the remotest part of the ranch. She recalled the vividness of his blue eyes, their boldness because he knew what no one else knew: that Jenny Wakefield was not as demure and perfect and virginal as everyone believed.

Everyone said that Blade was bad. Maybe he was, but he had made her feel wild with a kind of reckless exhilaration that both addicted and petrified her. That wickedness within her had ensnared her, and given him his power over her.

She remembered the way Blade's tousled gold hair had fallen across his brow as he lay on top of her, his bronzed, tough body intimately possessing hers, easing himself ever so gently inside her, stealing her virginity. He had stared deeply into her eyes with an intense male possessiveness before he lowered his head to take her lips, kissing her again, more tenderly than before, perhaps more tenderly than he had ever kissed any woman. But there was anger in him as well. In those days there had always been anger in Blade.

"Remember *this,* preacher's daughter, when you lie with my brother in your marriage bed," he'd taunted softly. She'd tried to resist him then, but he'd moved his body so that wave after wave of spiraling thrills coursed through her. He'd taught her so thoroughly the rapture of what it was to be a woman and know a man that the memory of that hazy golden afternoon still burned within her.

Later, when she'd shyly sought him in all the places on

the Zachery Ranch where he could usually be found, he was conspicuously absent, and she'd realized with a pang of terrible remorse that he was deliberately avoiding her.

Did he think her cheap and easy because of the way she'd wanted him? The way she'd reveled in his love-making? The way she'd moaned in that last moment of total surrender?

Had she, sweet Jenny Wakefield, the preacher's daughter, really bitten him on the neck and given him that terrible bruise? She'd been mortified, but he'd only laughed and said gently, "It's only a hickey, Jenny. I'll just button my collar way up high the way you do 'til it goes away if it makes you feel so bad."

Then he'd kissed her, and she'd forgotten her shame in the glory and tenderness of his kiss.

Dean had off-handedly supplied information concerning his brother's whereabouts. "Don't know where in the hell that good-for-nothing brother of mine has gone this time, and just when we need him to work the cattle. Probably holed up with a bottle of whiskey and some woman he's got a yen for in some cheap hotel. He's as sorry as his real old man was. But you know Pa. No matter what Blade does, he can't see the bad in him. He's forever throwing Blade up to me, the way he breaks his back working on the ranch, the way he understands animals, the way he stands up to people who try to push him around. It's not like Blade, though, to disappear like this when Pa needs him. He's usually smart when it comes to Pa. Wonder what it was that drove him away."

Jenny had wondered if Blade were running from her. Did he despise her for what she had done? Was that why he'd said he wanted nothing to do with her as long as she was determined to marry his brother?

Blade had made no promises to her, no declarations of love, but he'd asked her not to marry Dean.

Two days later she'd married Dean Zachery, telling herself that it was just a craziness inside her that had driven her into Blade's arms, that it was Dean she really loved; Dean, who'd been her childhood playmate, her high school sweetheart; Dean, who was gentle and kind; Dean, who was the sort of man who made a good husband. The Jenny Wakefields of the world didn't marry fast, loose men like Blade Taylor, men who drank and chased women and lived as if there were no tomorrow. She'd known that she had to suppress the unholy wildness within her at all costs, and the only way she knew how was to marry Dean.

The whole town remembered Jamie Taylor, Blade's father, whose love of drink had blurred his rugged good looks even before middle age. His blue eyes had grown vacant, his virile physique fleshy. He'd turned shiftless, losing his animals one by one to neglect, finally losing the small ranch he'd inherited. His wife had grown tired of his beatings, and she'd run away with a man she'd met in the local bar, leaving Jamie and her small son behind. One night two years later, after a week-long drinking spree, Jamie had come home, and while he lay smoking in bed he'd set the house on fire. Blade had been ten the night his father died. Everyone in town remembered the pitiful, fatherless little boy, and how lost he'd seemed after the death of his only relative. But only one person had cared enough to do something about him.

Caleb Zachery had adopted the boy and tried to raise him decently. After that Blade's clothes were clean, his hair washed and combed. For the first time, everyone noticed his sultry good looks, and whispered that such sex appeal in one so young was dangerous. And for a while some of the bitterness left the boy. Blade worked hard on the ranch for Caleb, as Dean, who preferred to read books and dream grand dreams, would not. For a time there were those who even believed that the boy might amount to something someday. But as he grew older, his father's wildness had become evident in him. By the time he was seventeen he was not amused by such innocent pursuits as school dances and football games. It was said that he drank too much, and that the females he preferred were women, not girls.

"Bad blood will out," the townspeople all agreed. "Blade Taylor will end up just like his father."

Jenny had married Dean more out of terror than because she loved him; she was terrified of her own feelings, of what she'd done. Of what she might do again if Blade Taylor cast those smoldering blue eyes upon her and made her remember the ecstasy of his embrace. Ever since she was a small child, Jenny had tried to be perfect, and with Dean, the task of being the good person she believed she should be seemed almost easy.

She'd spent every day of her marriage trying to make up to Dean for the one transgression of her life, but no matter what she did, it never seemed enough. She'd slept with his adopted brother, the only person that gentle Dean had ever disliked. If he had ever found out, it would have destroyed him.

She and Dean had lived together for eight years, and Dean had never known the wanton Jenny that Blade had touched. Their sex had lacked the dangerous excitement she'd experienced with Blade, if only that once, and when Dean made love to her, Jenny had traitorously longed for Blade. She knew it was wrong, but she'd wanted to feel again that mad, blind passion that turned her emotions inside out and left her spent and aching and limp as jelly. If after their lovemaking she was more thoughtful and attentive to her husband than usual out of guilt, Dean had cockily attributed her behavior to his prowess as a lover.

Oh, the wickedness of her deceit!

"Perfect in every way," Mike had said, describing her. Mike didn't know her any better than Dean had. Thank heaven he didn't. Thank heaven no one did.

"You haven't heard a word I've said," Mike chided gently, interrupting the chaos of her thoughts and returning Jenny abruptly to the present. "All that financial expertise wasted."

She gripped the receiver in sudden awareness.

"Sorry. My mind was a million miles away."

"What I was saying is that we're going to have to hold off on that land sale."

"Why, Mike? You know I need the capital for the resort."

Normally she would have caught the strange edge to his voice. Today she was too upset. "Perhaps it's a mistake to throw good money after bad, Jenny. That ranch land is going up in value every year. It's something I feel you should hang on to. The resort's been losing money steadily."

"Mike, I have to have the money."

"I've managed to get a loan with very generous terms for you. For now, at least, you don't have to sell anything."

"Oh, Mike that's wonderful!"

"Yes, isn't it?" Again there was something in his voice that should have warned her.

"The resort was so important to Dean. I just have to keep it going for him."

21

"Dean's been dead two years, Jenny. Maybe it's time you stopped living in the past."

"I'm trying, but sometimes . . . you know, today—" She couldn't continue.

"Yes, I know."

"It's funny how a date on the calendar brings back the past."

"Funny, and then not so funny."

"Mike, I don't think I'm handling myself too well today."

"You're doing fine. I know it's not easy. Dean was a part of your life; losing him was like losing a part of yourself. It's going to take time. You two had the perfect storybook love. I used to be so jealous of Dean because he had you. Only the ending wasn't happily ever after."

"Yes," she said softly, "the perfect storybook love."

If only he knew.

The man who knew stood on the side of Ranch Road 12, his Marine Corps duffel bag lying on the dusty gravel beside his varnished boots. At the sight of a lone car in the distance he lifted his thumb and signaled. Not that Blade Taylor expected the car to stop. Hitchhiking took a while these days. The whole country was paranoid from an oversaturation of media violence. People saw the possibility of murder, rape, and assault in the eyes of every stranger, even in the clean-cut looks of a former Marine Corps officer who stood lean and tall in his crisp shirt and stiffly creased Levi's.

There was no bus service to Zachery Falls, and when he'd reached San Marcos there had been no one in Zachery that Blade felt easy about calling. He wasn't exactly the town's favorite hero. Caleb was dead. There was only Jenny, and she despised him. Not that he blamed her, after what he'd done, and that only a day or two before her marriage to his brother. Some brother. He and Dean had never liked each other, not even before Caleb had been generous enough to adopt Blade. Still, Jenny hadn't deserved the way Blade had treated her, as if she were common and easy and his for the taking—but what experience had he had with girls such as Jenny back then? His women had always been wild and willing, women who had such a yen for loving that they'd let any man love them. How could he have understood a woman like Jenny? She'd been a virgin, and before her, for all his experience, he'd never had a virgin.

The red sports car whizzed jauntily past Blade, and he lowered his thumb. He hadn't expected it to stop. Suddenly there was the squeal of brakes, and the car began to back up. Blade leaned down and picked up the duffel bag, slung it over his wide shoulder, and strode toward the car, his steps long and easy. He moved like a man who'd grown sure of himself over the years.

Shoulder-length blond hair ruffled over the edge of the bucket seat, and Blade's sensual mouth curved cynically. A woman. It had been a long time since he'd had a white woman who was free and willing. In the Middle East the only women a Marine could have were bought and sold.

"Blade?" The velvet voice was uncertain.

"Well, I'll be damned! Susan Harper!" Blade caught himself. "Excuse the language, Susan. I've just gotten my discharge papers from the Marines. It may take me a while to remember how to act with a lady."

"You never had any trouble knowing how to act with a woman in the past, Blade Taylor," she teased, her tone silkily suggestive. "Don't tell me you were wounded somewhere . . . important." Her hot eyes roamed over his virile physique.

"Good Lord, no!"

She laughed deliciously and leaned forward to light a cigarette.

She was so beautiful. He couldn't even remember when he'd last been with a woman, but as Blade stared down at the girl in the bucket seat, her platinum head tipped at a coquettish angle, he was not thinking of her. Instead he saw Jenny as he'd seen her that last time at Dean's funeral, in her loose black dress with her long brown hair swept away from her face. Her gentle expression had been filled with pain. Blade had wanted to take her in his arms that day, to kiss her, to soothe away her anguish, to make her forget Dean. Sometimes it seemed that all his life he'd wanted only one thing—for Jenny Zachery to forget Dean. He wanted that badly, but Blade Taylor was a man who'd grown up knowing what it was to do without the things he wanted.

Instead of comforting Jenny that day, Blade had done the only thing he knew to help. He'd walked out of her life before the temptation to stay made it impossible for him to leave her again. In the two years since then, her face had haunted him, tempted him—and he'd never been one to resist temptation for long. So here he was, back in Zachery Falls, wishing that Jenny would just once look at him the way Susan Harper was looking at him now, with her eyes warm and soft and yet suggestive. What would it take to make Jenny look at him like that? Idly he wondered if Susan knew what glances like that did to men. Of course she did. The Susan Harpers of the world always knew what they did to men.

He opened the door and swung his duffel bag into the

space behind the seats. Then he levered his long, lean body into the car.

"Big man, little car," she murmured, her eyes appraising the length of him.

"It beats walking. Thanks, Susan, for the lift."

"My pleasure." Again there was a suggestive element in her words.

"I'll have to find a way to repay you."

"That'll be easy, Blade. Real, real easy."

She tilted her pack of cigarettes toward him and he took one, leaning his golden head toward hers, lighting his cigarette from the tip of hers, his warm brown fingers steadying her wrist as he did so.

"Hmmmm. You smell good, Blade. Clean and all male."

He merely smiled at her in that easy way of his and leaned his head back against the seat, inhaling deeply. It felt surprisingly good to be with someone he knew.

The wind was springtime cool and scented with cedar and all the things he remembered growing up with. He hadn't known he'd missed all this so much. The sun was brilliant, but not hot. It was a glorious day to be coming home, and for the first time in a long while he felt some of his anxiety slipping away from him.

The wind rumpled his golden hair and blew it back from his tanned face. His military haircut was growing out, and his hair now reached his crisp blue collar. He cast his vivid blue eyes upon Susan and inhaled again. The cigarette tasted good. Too damned good. He supposed it was from doing without. He was reminded of other pleasures he'd been doing without. Again he thought of Jenny and the prim-and-proper virtue that had driven him so crazy all those years ago. He smiled. It wasn't only her prim-and-proper virtue that could drive him crazy, but the memory of that time when she'd melted against his body and become a woman.

"I'm trying to quit, you know," he said, his deep voice lazy. "You always were a girl to tempt a man from the path of the straight and narrow." He laughed softly, intimately.

"Was I? I'm glad you didn't forget me, Blade. I certainly never forgot you."

"Really?" A faintly cynical edge had crept into his speech. "Whatever happened to old Bill? You and he were pretty hot, last I heard."

"I divorced 'old' Bill a year ago."

"Kids?"

"Two. He's got them, except for every other weekend."

"Why?" Blade was no longer staring at Susan but at the road whipping past.

"I travel."

"A traveling saleswoman?" Again he laughed. "That's a switch."

"It's not as bad as it sounds."

"I was hoping it was."

This time she laughed.

"What about you, Blade? Married?"

"No."

"That sounds final. But they always said you weren't the marrying kind."

"Yes, that's what they always said—among other things."

"Were they right?"

"Maybe."

It felt damned good to be coming home. It was lucky, Susan recognizing him on the road.

"Anybody ever tell you that you drive too fast, Susan?"

"Lots of people tell me I'm fast, Blade. You used to like that in a woman."

"Oh, I still do." Again he was thinking of Jenny, wondering how she'd look when he saw her again. What would she say? How would she feel? He wished he could tease her the way he teased Susan.

"How come you're coming back to Zachery Falls, Blade? You've got no family here to hold you, and you're not exactly a favorite in town."

Blade shrugged. "I came back because there's something here I want."

Susan tossed her head and stared at him, and her hair flew against his shoulder. "You must want it very badly to brave the town's hatred, when there's a whole world out there just waiting."

"As a matter of fact, I do."

"Gonna tell me about it?"

"No."

"Blade—"

"Susan, let's just leave things as they always were between us—light and easy. Maybe you should look up old Bill. It's bad when a couple splits up and there are kids involved. I should know."

At his rejection, Susan looked hurt. "Okay, Blade."

He heard the funny catch in her voice, and he said. "But that doesn't mean we can't be friends. We always were, you know. Why don't you let me take you to lunch at the Bluebonnet Café? I owe you for the ride. You can fill me in on what's been going on in Zachery Falls while I've been away."

"Could we talk somewhere more private first?"

"Why don't you pull over onto that back road that winds down to the creek? Do you remember the place where the oaks and cypresses grow real close to the water and the grass grows long?"

"Of course I do."

Susan swerved and the car skidded on two tires as she made the turn. When she stopped in the deep shade beneath the spreading branches of a live oak, they each lit another cigarette. The cool woodsy smell of the creek and the scent of wild flowers made Blade remember Jenny, and the one time he'd made love to her. Susan began talking, and at first he only half listened. He was thinking of brown hair coiled over his hand, brown hair tangled with the sweetness of wild flowers.

"Blade, you seem different now."

"In what way?"

"There's an easiness about you. I don't know . . . I can't quite put my finger on it. You're more self-confident, I guess, instead of angry. You used to be mad all the time, Blade."

"I did, didn't I? But back then I thought I had a whole lot to be mad about."

"What's everybody going to think of you now, the way you've changed? Imagine, Blade Taylor growing up and losing his wildness and amounting to something after all. You know what some folks will say? That maybe Caleb left you something in his will. Now wouldn't that just give everybody in Zachery Falls something to think about?"

Blade stiffened, his expression darkening at the mention of Caleb. But when he spoke his voice was still easy. "I suppose it would, but why don't you tell me what happened with you and old Bill, Susan?"

Susan began to talk, and she didn't even notice how smoothly he had changed the subject from himself to her.

They talked for a long time, and Blade listened with compassion. Susan didn't know that he was wishing that he and Jenny Zachery could talk like this, easily and in friendship. But there had never been anything easy about Jenny Zachery.

He pushed thoughts of Jenny from his mind. For now it was enough to be home, to be with someone who had once been his friend.

He prodded Susan with questions and forced himself to concentrate on her answers even though he had something far more important that he needed to do.

For the moment he allowed himself to forget the reason he had come back to Texas, the reason that would come as a shock to everyone in Zachery Falls, especially Jenny.

There would be time enough to claim what had long been rightfully his.

2

Did you hear the news? Blade Taylor's back in town."
It was a whisper that spread like the wind, stirring the
flimsy cypress leaves, rippling across the river's smooth
surface, blowing coolly into half-opened windows, reaching everywhere, everyone.

Gossip spread like lightning in a town the size of
Zachery Falls. As soon as Susan's red Porsche swerved
around the last curve before the long bridge over the
Blanco River, where Clay Hammock was fly-fishing that
Wednesday afternoon, people began to talk.

There was no one except Blade with hair that precise
shade of deep gold, the rich color of leaves in the Texas
hill country's late autumn. No one with hair that was so
untidy. What was it about him that made one always
imagine that it was a woman's fingers that had rumpled it,
as she lay beneath him in passion? Leave it to Blade to
find a woman before he even hit the city-limit sign. But

then, if the woman was Susan Harper, it figured. Blade and she had always been two of a kind.

When Jenny heard the news she was in the hardware store, where she'd gone to speak to Don Wilkerson about buying some chain link to fence an area behind her house so that Cathy could play outside without someone having to watch her every second.

Two women were behind a shelf that held spice racks and other kitchen knickknacks. Their voices were tantalizingly low as they spoke. Jenny, for all her surface virtue, was only human. She stepped closer to the shelf.

"Blade Taylor's back. Seen him in the Bluebonnet Café with Susan Harper. Looks like the two of them already got something going again."

"Wonder why he came back? He can't be up to anything good. Never was, you know. And he never liked Zachery Falls much, if I remember."

"Never could understand what Caleb Zachery saw in him."

"Some things are hard to figure."

"Handsome devil. So big and tall. It's plain enough to see why women swarm around him even if he is no good."

"Won't get them anywhere. A man like him can't help but break a woman's heart."

"Just like his father, if you ask me. And you know what happened to him."

Jenny forgot what she'd been meaning to ask Don about the chain link when he came back from the warehouse. She was shaking with a mixture of turbulent emotions. Blade was back, and he was with Susan Harper in the Bluebonnet Café. She trembled and caught her breath. Odd, how it hurt, to think of Blade with Susan. Then, as Jenny continued listening, her first chaotic feelings changed to angry indignation.

Those two old biddies, Katey Scudder and Margaret Harris, had no right to talk about Blade like that. A big part of the trouble with Blade was that no one in Zachery Falls had ever given him a chance to be anything but bad. Jenny was about to storm around the high shelf and confront the two women, but she managed to stop herself in the nick of time.

What would they think if she rushed down upon them as angrily as a maddened hornet—the virtuous Jenny Zachery attacking two of the town's most respected matrons, defending her bad brother-in-law? Would it be all too evident that she wasn't so different from the Susan Harpers of the world? And why was she defending Blade, if only to herself?

"Because he *needs* someone to defend him," she shouted silently, even as another inner voice mocked her. *You're still as bad as ever, Jenny Zachery. Nothing ever changes. Not in people's hearts and souls. Not in towns like Zachery Falls.*

So she contained her outrage, lest they suspect the reasons that lay behind it, but it felt horrible to be such a hypocrite.

Two days passed, and the buzzing about Blade slowed down, even though no new and more interesting topic of gossip had presented itself. Jenny threw herself into her work harder than ever before. The contractor had finished remodeling ten of the lodge rooms in time for the summer rush. She needed to see about having the pool repainted, and she had to purchase new outdoor furniture. That last would require a trip to San Antonio. There were a few more details that the contractor had to take care of before she could write him a final check. The baseboards weren't painted, he'd failed to install electrical outlets in the bathrooms, and some of the carpeting was improperly laid. Then there was the new chef she needed to hire.

The Zachery Falls pay scale was not the best in the world, but it was difficult to convince the men who came from larger cities to interview for the job that in a small town things didn't cost as much, either. All the men could see was the smaller salary.

Between taking care of Cathy and running the resort, Jenny baked four dozen cookies for the church social. She found time to help decorate the church parlor as well. But even though she kept herself virtuously busy, her mind was a mad tumble, and Blade Taylor was at the center of that tumble.

Why didn't he at least come out and say hello? Hadn't he grown up on the Zachery ranch? Wasn't he sentimental at all? Had he completely forgotten Caleb? But, of course, what she really wondered was, had he forgotten her?

It was all too obvious that he had. She had been no more than a romp in the hay—and his life had been a continual romp. It was doubtful that he even remembered her. There were probably too many beautiful, experienced women in his past.

Oh, to be a man! For an instant she allowed herself to envy Blade for the wild life he had led. To be free. Not to have to be so everlastingly good! It wasn't fair, the way society chained women, but let men run loose to tempt them from their chains. If women let themselves fall to temptation, they were wicked, wicked creatures. Despite all the talk about women's liberation, in Zachery Falls nothing had really changed.

So it was a thoroughly confused Jenny Zachery who looped her arm through Mike Kilpatrick's expensively suited one and let him escort her to the church social. Cathy toddled ahead of them down the long sidewalk to his sleek blue Cadillac that Friday evening.

Mike was so nice, so safe. He was just the sort of man she should marry, just the sort who would be good to her, and to Cathy, as well. Why, then, did she yearn to see Blade again?

It was midnight when they returned to the ranch. Cathy was asleep in Jenny's arms. Mike's hand rested comfortably on Jenny's shoulder as he parked in front of her limestone ranch house. When he bent his head and took her mouth in gentle possession, Cathy squirmed and began to cry.

Jenny pulled away and cradled the child more closely against herself to make her hush. "I'm sorry, Mike." But she wasn't, not really.

"That's okay," he said, his voice filled with the infinite patience that Jenny admired in him. "She's exhausted from being the belle of the ball."

"Wasn't she a little doll?" Jenny murmured proudly, remembering the way Cathy had run to everyone and laughed and gurgled so charmingly. "Sometimes she can be so sweet." Cathy began to kick and scream in earnest. "Like I said, sometimes."

Mike laughed as he got out of the car and went around to open the passenger door.

As Jenny stepped out onto the drive holding the writhing child, she noted for the first time that there was a light on in the apartment above the garage, the apartment Blade had lived in so long ago. The light hadn't been on when they'd left.

That apartment was where she stored retired files. Chuck must have taken a box up there and forgotten to turn the light off, she decided, thinking that she would have to see to it later. That would be just like Chuck.

"Come on in, Mike," Jenny said at the front door, "and I'll make you some coffee after I put Cathy to bed."

"I'll come in, but you can skip the coffee. I got enough at the social. I'll probably be up the rest of the night from all the caffeine."

"You should have had the punch."

"I've never really been much of a punch drinker."

Jenny disappeared into Cathy's room to help the little girl slip into her nightgown and get ready for bed. Cathy was holding her blanket and sucking her thumb with fierce determination. Some of the ladies at the social had been quite severe in their advice when they'd found out that Cathy enjoyed her thumb so much.

"She's only two," Jenny had defended.

"My Lottie had quit well before she was two," Lois had stated smugly. "You should paint her thumb. That will make her stop."

In Zachery Falls people were interested in the most minute details of other people's lives. It really was amazing the way they were so quick to pass judgment. Jenny often found herself thinking defiantly. "I wish I were like Blade and didn't care about other people's opinions. How nice that would be." But she had always cared. And she probably always would.

Mike was waiting as patiently as always when she returned. She walked over to him. "The little monster is asleep."

"At last." He chuckled. "At long last, I have you to myself." He pulled her down onto the sofa, capturing her mouth with his.

She returned his kiss dutifully, wishing that he would stir her in a way that he never had before. But even though his kiss was long and hard, even though he was handsome and not an inexperienced lover, his embrace evoked none of the savage hunger she longed to feel.

"I want you to marry me, and soon," he said, pulling away, breathing hard. "I don't know how much more of this I can stand. I know you too well to expect you to sleep with me before marriage. You're not the kind of woman who goes to bed with a man without making a permanent commitment."

Oh, wasn't she? Rebelliously she wished she weren't locked into such a virtuous mold, but then she knew she didn't wish that at all. Not really. It was kind of nice, people thinking better of you than you really were. It made life easier sometimes. Then she remembered the strange restlessness that came upon her at times, and she knew that it could make life harder, too. You couldn't run away from the secrets locked away in your own soul.

"Hold me, Mike," she said. "Just hold me. I feel so afraid. I don't know myself these days. I don't know what I really want. I don't know what to do."

"Simple. Marry me. I'll take over the resort and the operation of the ranch. You know I already love Cathy, and I've always loved you, Jenny."

But that wasn't what she'd meant. Not at all.

She stared at him in silent anguish, and he offered her the only comfort that he could. He held her in the darkness until, much later, she fell asleep in his arms. Very gently he released her and laid her head back upon the couch. Covering her with an afghan, he bent and kissed her brow, leaving her and walking out the front door, locking it behind him.

She woke when she heard the bolt click, realizing that

he had gone and she was alone. She got up and went to her bedroom. Her window shades were raised, and the light from the garage apartment glared brightly, making her wish she'd remembered to ask Mike to see about it before he left. Well, she'd take care of it herself, before she went to bed.

Blade heard Jenny's light footsteps coming up the stairs, and he pulled the sheet and blankets over his bronzed, naked body, which was still damp from his shower.

Oh, Lord. Kilpatrick must have left. Not that Blade was sorry about that. He'd hated the dark house and the car in front hour after hour. He'd hated the thought of Jenny alone with Mike. Still, Blade had hoped that he wouldn't have to face Jenny until the morning. He was exhausted from the long hours he'd spent cleaning up the apartment and making it habitable again. Jenny was certainly a pack rat, the way she'd stuffed this place so full of boxes that he could hardly move around. It had taken him most of the night to carry all that junk down to the garage.

The thought of seeing her again, the thought of explaining what he was going to do made him feel uneasy.

Jenny stepped into the room, realized she wasn't alone, and screamed.

"I should be the one to scream," Blade said lightly, with one of his easy, white smiles. "I always thought that ladies like you knocked before they entered a man's bedroom. You know, I'm not wearing a stitch, and my clothes are hanging on that chair. If I get up to put something on and get decent—"

"D-don't get up!" she cried, shamefully aware of that long, forbidden male body outlined beneath sheet and blanket. Her awareness made her tremble and caused her skin to go hot, and she hoped frantically that he didn't see how he affected her.

"Blade, I . . . I saw the light, and I only came up to turn it off. I never thought I'd find you here."

He smiled teasingly. "That's obvious. But I'm glad to see you, Jenny. Come on in. You know I never was a man not to be glad about a midnight visit from a beautiful woman, especially my own dear sister-in-law."

She went scarlet, and he wished he hadn't said that. What devil drove him to taunt her when he knew how it always embarrassed her? He had never known how to act around her—probably because she was the only woman who'd ever been special to him.

Lord, she looked pretty, even prettier than he remembered. Her lipstick was smudged, probably from Kilpatrick's kisses, but she was still in the same clothes she'd put on for the church social. It was incredible that Kilpatrick could have been in that dark house for hours without making love to her. Blade was grateful for that, but he was baffled. No doubt Jenny liked that sort of gentlemanly treatment, but how did a man like Kilpatrick keep his sanity?

She was wearing a white lace dress with long puffed sleeves, the cotton fabric so thin that he could see her arms beneath it. The dress was high necked, of course, and every tiny button was fastened clear up to her throat. A tiny golden cross twinkled at her collar.

It was not the kind of dress, nor the sort of jewelry that the more voluptuous Susan would have worn, but he liked them on Jenny. He liked the way the dress outlined her small breasts and her narrow waist; he liked the way the soft folds of material flowed over her hips and down past her knees. He didn't want her to wear dresses that revealed her body to other men. Ever since he'd made love to her that once, he'd known that he wanted her forever. And he didn't want anyone else to have her, even if only in their minds. Not anyone. Not Dean. Not Kilpatrick. As he thought of Kilpatrick, it occurred to Blade that he'd returned just in time.

It had almost killed him when Jenny had gone ahead and married Dean all those years ago. How he had hated Dean for that. He couldn't help himself. Dean had always had everything Blade had wanted so badly for himself. Dean had been Caleb's rightful son, the rightful heir to the ranch that Blade had loved and worked. The blood of Jamie Taylor did not taint the pure, self-righteous Dean Zachery.

From childhood Dean had held the town's respect and love, while they'd looked upon Blade with scorn and considered him trash. He wasn't trash, but if it hadn't been for Caleb's believing in him and adopting him, he might have turned out that way. Not that anyone in Zachery Falls would have cared.

If it hadn't been for Caleb, Blade wouldn't have stuck through college for five years. And he certainly never would have made it through officer candidacy school. In the ten years Blade had spent away from Zachery Falls, he'd learned that he wasn't trash. The people he'd met in faraway places, people who didn't know about Jamie Taylor and his drunkenness, had respected Blade for the man he was and had judged him on the merits of what he did.

Blade remembered the night Dean had married Jenny. He had wanted to die that night. He'd gone to Caleb and told him what he'd never admitted to anyone, not even to himself—that he loved Jenny, that he'd always loved her, since they were kids. He couldn't stay at the ranch,

knowing that she belonged to Dean. Caleb had understood, and sent him off to college.

Maybe that wasn't the only reason Caleb had made it
so easy for Blade to go away and stay away. Maybe
Caleb had seen the way Jenny would look at Blade when
Dean wasn't around and she didn't think anyone saw
her. That was why Blade had taken her the way he had,
because he'd felt the fire in those soft green eyes too
often to stay his desire. Maybe she hadn't known what
she was doing when she'd looked at him like that, but
when he'd made love to her on that long ago afternoon
in a bed of sweet-smelling wild flowers, she'd been more
responsive than he could ever have dreamed.

Yes, Caleb had understood about a lot of things that
other people never understood, especially not his thick-
headed son, Dean. Dean had married Jenny, but he had
never really known her.

Sometimes Blade thought that if it hadn't been for
Caleb Zachery and his love and understanding, the deep,
wild anger that had driven him ever since his childhood
would have destroyed him. Blade himself believed that
there was something bad within him, something he'd
been born with, the same bad element that had destroyed his father and made his mother desert him and
run off. But there was something else within him as well,
an inner determination to rise above the bad. Caleb
Zachery had seen the potential in the bitter ten-year-old
orphan who had hated the world and everyone that
inhabited it. The only other person during those early
years who had ever been kind to Blade was Jenny.

Dean and Jenny and Blade were all exactly the same
age, and they were in the same grade in school when
they were growing up. When Blade was only six years

old, the other children had laughed when he had come to school with a black eye because Jamie had thrown a chair at him. His clothes had been torn, and he'd been without a lunch box. But Jenny hadn't laughed. She'd packed an extra sandwich for him and brought it the next day. Blade had been too proud and embarrassed to take it when she'd so shyly offered it to him. He refused her roughly with all the clumsy anger a six-year-old boy can show a little girl, and she'd run off crying. He'd felt so awful about that later, making her cry. He hadn't known what to do. He'd thought and thought about it, mulling over the wonder of her making it for him, the marvel of her thinking about him. It was a kindness he never forgot—but then, he didn't have many kindnesses to remember.

In the fifth grade, right after Jamie had died and before Caleb had officially adopted him, Blade had been in the school cafeteria when he'd overheard Kelly Robinson holding court with the other girls, sniggering about him behind the soda machine.

"That Blade Taylor's so mean and nasty. The way he looks at you, with all that hate. The way he always gets in trouble. He's just trash. Pure, plain old trash, that's what my mama says. I wish he'd drop dead." That had been the pious Kelly speaking, and her opinion was usually law among all the girls in her clique.

Blade had hated the whole world when he heard that. He'd wanted to do something awful just to scare Kelly and make her sorry for what she'd said. But to his amazement, Jenny's timid voice had rushed to defend him.

"I don't think Blade's bad. He's just lonely, not having a family like the rest of us, not knowing what's going to

41

happen to him. It must be awful for him. How would you feel if your mother ran away and your father burned up and you were left all alone?"

"How would you know so much about Blade Taylor, Jenny Wakefield?" the others sneered, their voices nasty and suggestive.

"That's what I think, no matter what you say." There had been tears in the shy voice. "If you would only give him a chance, he might be nicer."

Maybe that was the day that Blade had started loving her, but it had been a secret emotion locked deep within himself. Only once had he nearly given his feelings away.

They'd been in the tenth grade then. Grades were always important to Jenny, and biology was her worst subject. Blade sat right behind her in that class. She must have been desperate because she'd carried a cheat sheet into the final, and since she wasn't really a cheater, she hadn't known how to manage it as suavely as the more blasé, habitual cheaters of Blade's acquaintance. She'd been nervous and scared and in her confusion she'd dropped the incriminating paper onto the floor. It had landed so conspicuously that Mr. Jeffries had marched down the aisle and retrieved it.

"Jenny." The teacher's voice was cold and unforgiving, and Blade had hated the way Jenny looked so pale and cowed. "Young lady, do you know what cheating on a final exam means?"

It meant an F in the course.

Jenny was too terrified to speak. The whole class was staring at her. She'd never been in trouble before.

Blade hadn't even thought. He'd just reacted. He jumped out of his chair with a defiant swagger. "It wasn't her, Mr. Jeffries. It was me," he'd said in that sullen, disrespectful voice that all the teachers hated. "I stole her notes."

"Blade." Jenny had begun a weak attempt to save him.

"Shut up, Jenny. You always were such a sissy. I should have let him pin it on you."

"All right, Taylor. That's just the sort of thing I'd expect out of you."

He'd been expelled for three days; he'd also received an F in biology and a stern lecture from Caleb, but he hadn't minded because Jenny had come all the way out to the ranch herself to thank him.

He'd been repairing a barbed wire fence when she'd found him. She'd gotten off her horse slowly, shyly, and he'd noticed how slim and cute she was in her jeans, how clean and fresh she smelled, how pretty she was with her hair blowing loose about her face.

Impulsively, she'd reached out and touched him, and when she stepped closer, he couldn't stop his arms from going around her.

Her voice was choked and strange. "I want to thank you, Blade, for what you did. I feel so awful about you getting expelled." Suddenly she began to cry and the more she cried the more upset she became.

His arms tightened about her, and he cradled her against his chest. She felt so good, and it made him feel strong and manly to comfort her. It seemed to him that he had wanted this moment for as long as he could remember.

"I'll never, never try to cheat again. To think that I got you into such trouble," she managed between sobs.

"It doesn't matter. I've been in trouble before. What's one more time?"

His hands had stroked the silken brown hair. His shirt was partially unbuttoned, and he felt her hot tears on his bare chest. The warmth of her had filled him with an aching need. He realized that he had only to lower his head to take her lips, only to slide his hands up her slim waist and untuck her blouse so that he could caress her breasts, only to unzip her jeans to explore soft, feminine flesh. He envisioned her naked loveliness.

"Oh, Blade," she said softly. "Everyone's always said you're bad, but you're not. I always knew they were wrong."

Those words had brought him up short and stopped him from trying to take her then and there.

Her beautiful eyes were shining as she lifted her face to kiss him gratefully on the cheek.

But it wasn't his cheek that she'd kissed. He twisted his head, and it was his mouth that met hers. Funny, how she hadn't pulled away when he'd kissed her long and deeply, until the blood was pounding in his veins and her own pulse was beating just as jerkily. It was he who had been stunned by his loss of control, he who was afraid of what he might do if he didn't release her. He'd pushed her roughly away.

"I'm sorry," he'd muttered. "I never meant for that to happen."

She was tracing the edge of her swollen mouth with her fingertips. Her expression was oddly intense, and she was so beautiful it hurt somehow.

"That was my first kiss," she said in awe. And as she swung herself back onto her horse, she'd stunned him. "And you don't have to be sorry about that kiss, Blade Taylor, 'cause I'm not."

It was after that that she started looking at him with

those hot green eyes when no one else was around to see. He'd known that she was ashamed of the way she felt about him because she'd look down whenever he looked at her, and he'd left her alone because he respected her. Besides, she had always been Dean's girl, all through high school. And for all her sweetness in defending him when they were children, Blade had known that she was much too nice a girl to ever be interested in him the way he was interested in her. So he'd chased after wild girls, girls who were attracted to a guy with a bad reputation, and his reputation had only grown worse, widening the distance between Jenny and himself even farther.

If Blade was lost in the past, so was Jenny. She was staring at him hard, her eyes soft and luminous, her mind as filled with memories of him as his was of her—only she was embarrassed by her memories, just as she was embarrassed at being here like this with him. It seemed wanton, his lying there naked, with the soft sweetness of the spring darkness outside. They had only to turn out the light, to touch each other. He made her feel primitive, as if all that really mattered was that he was a man and she was a woman.

"What are you doing here, Blade?" she asked, her voice strange and tight.

"I figured you'd heard I was back, knowing the way people in Zachery Falls always talk."

"I heard, but that doesn't answer my question."

He plumped his pillow, and his action made the sheet fall to his waist, exposing his muscled, golden brown chest and flat belly. She couldn't drag her eyes from his body. A damp sheen clung to his golden hair. The smell of his masculine cologne drifted over her.

He was beautiful, sinfully beautiful, and doubtless he knew it. Why in the name of heaven didn't he pull up that sheet? But she couldn't very well ask him to, because it would let him know what looking at him was doing to her. She wanted to touch him. It had been a long time since she'd been with a man, and forever since she'd known the fulfillment of what had been for Blade only a careless embrace on a long-ago spring afternoon.

"Well, this is where I used to live," he said in that soft male voice that could make her shiver and feel so odd. "And it's where I'm going to live now. I've come home, Jenny. To stay."

"You . . . you can't be serious. What would people think? We can't live together." Then, realizing what she'd said and how it must have sounded to a man like him, her eyes widened in horror.

His hot blue eyes met hers. "Now there's an idea I never would have mentioned, not right off the bat, anyway—you and me living out here together. But I like it, Jenny Zachery. I like it much more than you could ever imagine. And as for what people think . . . well, you know that's one thing I never really gave much of a damn about."

His male gaze slid down her body as warmly as hands moving over her, reminding her of the way she'd felt in his arms that spring afternoon when he'd taken her virginity. He had no right to make her feel this way. She wanted to hate him for the power he held over her, for that easy power he had over all women.

"Any woman would do for you, Blade." Her voice was low. "I've heard all about Susan. The whole town knows."

"Knows what?"

"That you and she—"

"Yes?" He cocked his head and stared at her, a devilish light dancing in his eyes. She was blushing furiously. She never had been one who could get close to the subject of sex and handle it smoothly, and he'd always been one to taunt her.

"It's . . . it's certainly none of my business," she said huffily.

"I only wish that the rest of the town was as nobly indifferent to my business as you are."

"Susan said that you and she parked on the river road," Jenny blurted out.

The pain in her voice caught at his heart, and he stared at her hard, wanting to understand the reason for it. He was not so conceited that he didn't remember the way she'd felt about him, but it never occurred to him that she might be jealous. Blade had always thought when he was young that he wasn't good enough for her, and deep in his heart, for all his accomplishments since then, that's what he still thought.

He'd lived roughly, too roughly for a gentle woman like Jenny to ever understand or forgive, and then there were the horrors of Lebanon he still had to get over, the memories of death, of children . . . He pushed his mind away from the war and back to the woman standing near.

Ten years ago she'd been attracted to his aura of wildness, but then she'd seen her mistake and run headlong into marriage with Dean. Everyone had said that it was a perfect marriage. Blade had hated hearing that, but he'd believed it and felt ashamed for what he'd done to her right before her marriage, knowing that it must have made her hate him as all the other decent girls

47

had. She'd been saving herself for Dean—and Blade had always wondered about their wedding night. He still felt ashamed now, but guilt had a way of making him do things he regretted later. Sometimes he lashed out, instead of being tender.

His voice was cool and indifferent. "When was it wrong for two old friends to talk?"

"Is that all you did?" Again there was that odd pain in her voice that he was at a loss to understand.

"Would that be so difficult to believe?"

"People in Zachery Falls are saying that a man like you wouldn't be content with talk from a woman like Susan Harper."

"Is that what you believe?"

"Blade, you're deliberately confusing me. I don't know what to believe."

"Well, it's no concern of yours or anybody else's what Susan is to me. I told you the truth just a minute ago, but if you prefer the town's version, go right ahead and believe it."

"I—I don't prefer the town's version."

"Maybe you feel safer thinking I want Susan." He stared at her hard. "That's it, isn't it? You're afraid of me, aren't you, Jenny? Afraid of me wanting you?"

That thought made him hurt inside, and he tore his gaze from her stricken face. He felt even worse when she didn't deny it.

"Well, you're wrong there too, girl," he said roughly. "You don't have to worry about me getting any ideas about us just because of what happened that one time." Her sudden flush went through him like a knife, and his voice hardened with the guilt it made him feel. "That was a mistake and I know it, just as you know it. I know everybody around here thinks I'm some sort of sex maniac, but I'm not. I've never taken a woman who wasn't willing, and I'm not about to start now. I didn't move out here to embarrass you, either. This is my home. Just like it's yours. I hope we can be friends." He stopped speaking.

Jenny's mind screamed silently. *Oh, my God, he's really going to live out here.* Was there no way to stop him? Friends? How could she be friends with him? Didn't he know what just looking at him did to her?

She flung herself toward the door and pushed the screen open.

"Jenny." She raced blindly down the steps and he jumped from the bed, having forgotten that he was naked. "Jenny!"

But she was gone, and he thought better of going after her in the state he was in. He felt awful. He knew she didn't want him to stay, but he couldn't think of any way to make it easier for her because he hadn't the slightest intention of changing his mind. It was best to let her think about it and come to terms with it herself. And things weren't going to get any better tomorrow when she learned the reason why he'd come back. He was dreading that—telling her.

He lay down on the bed and thought of her, of how pretty she'd looked in that white dress. He fell asleep smiling, thinking of her.

In his dreams it was Jenny who'd picked him up when he was hitchhiking the other day on that ranch road, Jenny in her prim, white, schoolteacher dress.

They'd driven to that remote, private place where they'd made love all those years ago. He'd helped her from the car and watched her undress. Slowly, shakily, her fingers had loosened every button in that long row of buttons until her firm breasts were revealed. He'd slid the soft edges of her dress aside and kissed each nipple and darkened aureole long and slowly, until they were pouting and full.

When she'd come into his arms she'd made wild, wanton love to him with her tongue, kissing him everywhere, in places that women like Jenny Zachery never kissed a man. Then he'd taken her mouth with the savage need of a man long starved.

She climbed on top of him after a series of long, molten kisses, covering bronzed muscles with her long slim body, moving on him slowly and then more rapidly, undulating rhythmically, her soft moans of excitement arousing him even more than what she was doing because he wanted her to want him, to enjoy him. She'd smiled down at him, her face beautiful and soft. She wore the look of a woman deeply in love, and he'd taken her lips again, this time more gently. Then she knelt above him and took him in her mouth, her brown hair spilling over his stomach, her tongue loving him as his had once loved her, until his whole body felt as though it were on fire from the delicate manipulations of her mouth and tongue.

He awakened hot and shaking, his body throbbing, and he lay awake for a long time after that, perspiring, chastising himself for being an idiot. Nevertheless, despite the damn foolishness of it, he couldn't help thinking of her alone in her bed in that dark house, wishing he could go to her, longing for her to want him as he wanted her.

Thoughts like that were as crazy as his dream. Hadn't she run out as frightened as a rabbit at the mere thought of him living here? What would she do if he touched her, let alone tried to make love to her? He didn't think he could stand it if she shrank from him as though he were no better than dirt. But like everyone else in Zachery Falls, she probably felt he was trash, and that she was too good to be defiled by his lust.

Well, he'd show them. Damn it! He'd show Jenny Zachery, too.

3

~∙◦◦◦◦◦◦◦◦◦◦∙~

Blade had slept with the windows partially opened so that the familiar sounds and the sweet country scents of the ranch could seep inside. It felt good being back on Zachery Ranch, he thought as he woke up and stretched. He felt as though he belonged. Then he corrected himself. The ranch wasn't called that anymore, and no one in Zachery Falls but himself had ever thought he belonged.

He'd decided to get up early that first morning back on the ranch because there was something he wanted to do before he embarked on the mission that had brought him all the way from the Middle East.

The sun was just rising when he slid out of bed. A dove was cooing, and in the distance, a whippoorwill sang its woeful lament.

Blade shaved and dressed in clean, pressed Levi's and

a long-sleeved blue shirt that he left open at the throat. Shrugging into a suede jacket that emphasized the breadth of his wide shoulders and the slimness of his waist, he stepped into his boots and strode out the door, thinking about the way things had changed.

Woodlands Hideaway was the fancy name Dean had given to the development he'd begun when Caleb was scarcely cold in the ground. Dean had always been one to think big, and he hadn't been satisfied with simple ranching. He'd said that the time for profitable ranching in the Texas hill country was long past. He'd wanted to leave raising animals to the men with flat black land, where the grass grew long and lush. Ranching didn't belong in the exquisitely beautiful hill country with its emerald-clear rivers and bright blue skies. The topsoil was too thin from the overgrazing and farming of the past fifty years.

Dean had always said that the land outside of Zachery Falls was valuable because it was the hill country closest to Houston, only three hours from the giant metropolis. Not only that, but Zachery Falls was located between San Antonio and Austin, less than an hour from either of them, and those two cities were growing faster than any place else in the country.

As a result land prices were sky high around Zachery Falls, and climbing higher because city folks liked a break from the smog and traffic. They wanted to breathe fresh, dry air instead of that dank Houston stuff, and taste the beauty of country life in their spare time. The hill country was filling up with houses and developments. The tourist dollar had brought gold to the hills, and Dean wanted to mine some of that gold.

Dean had conceived his resort with the idea of creating

a country paradise for the city-weary tourist. With Woodlands Hideaway he'd wanted to bring the pleasures of the city to the slower pace of the country.

Blade hadn't agreed completely with Dean, although he'd seen some truth in his brother's argument. The ranch did need to be a profitable enterprise. And Blade was glad about one thing Dean had done—he'd located the development on the southern tip of the ranch on a high spot along the Blanco River. He'd taken Blade's advice and built the lodge, restaurant, nightclub, hotel accommodations, swimming pool, tennis courts, golf courses, country club, spa, and town houses in a cluster together on the Blanco, so that the rest of the ranch remained as it had always been, free of development. Caleb's original ranch house and garage, where Jenny and Blade now lived, were located on the northern corner of the ranch four miles from the resort. These buildings, set deep in the dark shade of juniper and oaks, were as secluded as ever.

Blade was glad of that; he was a man who liked wide, open spaces away from people. He'd learned early that people could crowd you when they didn't even have a mind to, and when they had a mind to, they could make life hell.

It was a mile walk through the thick juniper and scrub brush from the ranch house down to the cemetery, but Blade didn't mind. He wanted to walk the land, to get the feel of it under his boots again. He was careful of the prickly cactus as he stomped over the flat limestone rocks amid the scarlet clusters of Indian paintbrush, pink batches of primroses, and the masses of bluebonnets.

He loved spring in the hill country. It was the most beautiful time of the year, and it would always be special

to him because it was the season when he'd made love to
Jenny that once. As a boy, he'd never thought much
about all the flowers that covered the hill country every
spring—until that afternoon. But when he'd lain with her
slim, warm body crushed beneath his, he'd noticed how
beautiful the blossoms were next to her face, how sweet
they smelled, how fragile and lovely they were. She was
like that, too—sweet, fragile, and lovely. After that the
wild flowers had always made him think of her.

He startled an armadillo rooting among the rocks, and
a white-tailed deer flew ahead of him as the land sloped
down to the river. The cemetery was nestled in the dense
shade beneath a grove of ancient live oaks with the river
rustling alongside. The grave sites were cool even on the
hottest afternoons.

Blade paused at Dean's grave and then walked slowly
over to Caleb's. He stared for a long time at the simple
cross with Caleb's name engraved upon it.

Some men stood tall, and Caleb had been such a man.
A terrible sadness settled over Blade as he thought of the
heart attack that had taken Caleb so swiftly eight years
before. There hadn't been time to say good-bye, and
Blade had never been able to cry over the loss of the only
man he'd ever loved. The grief he felt still lay heavy in his
heart. Blade owed Caleb a debt he could never repay,
and he felt it keenly as he remembered the man who'd
adopted him.

Caleb had built the ranch from the little piece of land
his own father had left him during the Depression. He'd
added to it by ten-acre sections in the beginning, when
the land had been cheap. The ranch had meant so much
to Caleb; it had been his life's work. And now if Jenny,
out of loyalty to Dean's memory, were allowed to follow

the foolhardy course of selling acreage to pay the resort's debts, the ranch would dwindle to nothing in a tenth of the time it had taken Caleb to amass it.

"Building's hard, son; wrecking's easy." That's what Caleb had always said to Blade when he was in one of his rare talkative moods.

Caleb had been a builder, and his son Dean a dreamer. Blade was a practical man who played the hand life dealt him, the kind of man who could turn his brother's dream into a reality—because he had to.

Blade had come home, not only for himself, but because he'd at last seen a way to repay that old debt. He would save the ranch for Caleb's grandchild, even if it meant going against Jenny, the woman he had always loved.

"Blade." Behind him, Jenny's voice was soft and respectful. "I thought I might find you out here."

He turned, and there was the shyness in her face that had always appealed to him. She cast her eyes down as if she felt awkward and unsure about having came out to look for him. He liked the red sweater with its row of little white buttons and the skin-tight jeans she wore, and it took all of his willpower to drag his gaze from the shapely outline of her slim body.

"I'm sorry about last night, about the way I acted," she said, still with that shy note in her voice. "I'm afraid it wasn't much of a homecoming."

He smiled, thinking how nice of her it was to apologize. She looked so pretty, even if her hair was pinned up in that prim little bun. "I guess it was a better homecoming than I deserved," he said. What would she think if he did what he wanted to, if he went to her and pulled the pins from her hair so that it cascaded over her shoulders the way he liked it to, if he wound the gleaming strands through his fingers before he kissed her slowly on the mouth?

"I'd like to invite you to breakfast," she said. "It would save you from having to go into town."

"Now there's a real peace offering. I'd like that, Jenny. I'd like that very much."

"I took the jeep. Do you want a ride back to the house?"

He nodded, and followed her as she leaped agilely over the rocks down the face of the cliff to where the jeep was parked on the road. He couldn't help thinking how cute and rounded her hips were for so slim a woman.

He went around to the driver's side to open the door for her. He was conscious of her body, so close to his. He hesitated, towering over her. She seemed like such a little thing. Their eyes met, and neither could stop looking at the other.

"How've you been, Jenny," he asked gently, "since Dean died?"

For some reason the way he was looking at her, his manner so easy, his voice kind, brought back in a poignant rush all that she'd lost: Dean, the dreams of their youth, and her illusions about the kind of person she was.

Jenny felt like an idiot bursting into tears out on the road with the warm sun beating down upon them, but once she started, she couldn't seem to stop. All the pain she'd held inside her for so long began to flow out of her.

"Oh, Blade, it's been awful. I've been so lonely. And I haven't known what to do. Half the time I do everything wrong. I depended on Dean for everything, and since he's died, I haven't known what to do with myself. It's like I wasn't ever living for myself. I was living *his* life. And I feel like such a fool right now, bawling like this, when all you did was ask me a simple question. You don't want to hear about my problems." She sobbed more forlornly than ever, thinking how ridiculous it was that she felt so close to this man who'd been away so long.

Without thinking, Blade drew her into the hard circle of his arms. It was painfully obvious that she still loved Dean. But Blade wanted to hold her. He'd been aching to ever since he'd come back to Zachery Falls.

"There, there. Shh. I'm the fool. I should have known better than to ask you a stupid question like that. I ought to know what it's like to hurt so much inside that you're afraid to let it out for fear it'll consume you. I hurt so long myself I didn't know there was any other way you could feel. But maybe it's better for you to talk about it than to hold it all inside. I hate it when you cry, but if it'll make you feel better, you can cry all day for all I care." He stroked her hair. "Yes, Jenny, for you I'll just stand out here forever if that's what it takes. I'll even ignore my grumbling stomach and forget your sweet promise to cook my breakfast when I'm about half-starved," he said, trying to tease her out of her mood.

She knew what he was doing. "I'm trying to stop," she choked helplessly, but the tears kept flowing.

Gently he traced the trail of a tear down her soft cheek with one of his fingertips.

"That bad? Well, Dean was quite a guy. The whole town loved him. He had a good life. I think he had everything a man could need to be happy. He had you."

That made Jenny think of how she'd wronged Dean by yearning to be in another man's arms, and she continued weeping.

"You're probably upset because I came back," Blade said. "This is all my fault. I shouldn't have surprised you like that last night. I should have realized what a shock it would be.''

"Oh, no!'' she blurted, too distraught to deceive him. "I wanted you to come to the ranch. I felt awful when you didn't. I kept wondering where you were those two days when you didn't come, and they said you were with Susan Harper.'' Then, realizing what she'd admitted, she turned as scarlet as the Indian paintbrush blooming in bold, bright tufts at her feet.

If he didn't know better, he'd have thought she was jealous. But a woman like Jenny had no reason to be jealous of someone like Susan Harper, so he discarded that notion instantly. But there was pain in Jenny's face, and he knew he was responsible for it.

Suddenly she surprised him. "I'm glad you're back, Blade,'' she said passionately, and threw her arms around his neck. She pressed her body against his and hugged him tightly. "I don't feel so alone anymore.''

He felt her breasts rising and falling against his chest, her hands caressing his neck, touching the tendrils of gold that curled against the collar of his shirt, and he was terribly aware of her as a woman. She smelled so sweet, as if she'd just bathed. Her body fit his perfectly, and it made him remember that time he'd lain with her in the grasses beside Cypress Creek. The desire that rose in him seemed to be an almost unconquerable force, and the perspiration that broke out on his brow felt cold in the chilled air. He clenched his fists so tightly his nails dug into his palms.

It took all his willpower not to lower his mouth and taste the sweetness of her lips, but he knew that if he did, he wouldn't want to stop there. He wanted her. It seemed to him that he had longed for her for a lifetime. But a woman like Jenny wasn't anything like Susan. Jenny had thrown her arms around him because she wanted to be comforted, not because she wanted his hands all over her. She was used to nice men, like Dean and Mike Kilpatrick. It was living hell to try to be a gentleman, Blade thought. Lord knew he didn't have much experience in that role. But this moment with her was too special to ruin, and he would ruin it if he let his needs take over. For the first time in their long acquaintance she'd come to him as an adult seeking friendship and understanding. And damn, if it killed him, that's what he would give her.

Blade knew she didn't want his lovemaking. How would she react if she knew that her hips pressing against his loins made him feel wild enough to rip her clothes aside and carry her into the deepest part of the woods? He only knew how he would feel when her trust turned to disgust after he did that. He knew too well what it was to be treated as if he were dirt, and he hated that feeling. He didn't think he could stand it from Jenny.

So he stood leaning back against the jeep with her body pressing close, her long slim legs touching his, her breasts crushed against him, and he went on holding her until her sobs quieted. Even after that, when she didn't pull away, he held her, and his body was wracked with the delicious torture of his need. He felt torn apart by his conflicting desires, his physical arousal fighting with his wish to be the kind of man she wanted.

At last she tilted her head up, and her expression was shyly embarrassed. "I feel much better. Maybe all I needed was just to have a good cry."

Even with tears streaking her cheeks she was beautiful. Several of the buttons on her sweater had come undone, and he could see beneath the neckline. The bra she was wearing was transparent, and he saw the creamy, swollen smoothness of her breasts and the darkened tips of her nipples. He wanted to touch her, to caress her, to lower his mouth and lick the roseate tips of her breasts until they hardened. He wanted that badly.

"Thank you, Blade, for being so kind." Her face was luminous in its innocence.

"You're welcome, Jenny," he managed in a voice as dry as dust. Gently he disengaged her body from his.

Then he helped her into the jeep and walked around the back and swung himself inside next to her.

It was hell being a gentleman.

Odd, how tiny the kitchen seemed with Blade filling it, Jenny thought. His long legs were sprawled beneath the table as he drank his coffee and read the paper. Maria was in giving Cathy her bath, and the child's treble shouts could be heard in the background. She wanted to go see her Uncle Blade again.

When Blade had first come inside the house, he'd gone to Cathy's room, and the child, who was usually so shy with strangers, had thrown herself headlong into his arms, thumb plugged into her grinning mouth.

"You're a mighty big girl to be sucking your thumb so voraciously." He'd laughed.

Jenny had not laughed at that. Did even men like Blade Taylor think that all two-year-olds should be mature adults?

"Thumb," Cathy had cooed proudly, pulling it from her mouth and exhibiting it to him. He'd laughed again.

"You remind me of your grandpa, girl, with your dimples. And Caleb always was one to be proud of anything he did even when it wasn't so much. He'd have given anything to have known you, you know.'' He'd kissed her golden curls.

They'd played a while longer, the child and the man, before Maria had taken Cathy for fear that Blade's patience would wear thin. He was such a masculine man. It was amazing how gentle and patient he could be with a baby, Jenny thought.

She felt both excited and strange having him back. He was different, somehow. Surer of himself, and easier to be around. She didn't have the feeling that he might erupt at any moment the way he had when he was younger, though, come to think of it, he'd never erupted with her after that time in the first grade when she'd tried to give him a sandwich and unintentionally offended his pride. He'd always been nice to her.

Jenny tried to concentrate on the scrambled eggs and biscuits she was cooking, but her mind crept back to the wonder she'd felt when Blade was holding her. She'd never felt quite like that with Dean, even after ten years of marriage. She'd poured out her troubles to Blade, and his warmth and understanding had lifted them from her. Dean had always come to her with his problems, but he had had no time for hers. Jenny felt so close to Blade now, in some strange unfathomable way, closer than she'd ever felt to anyone.

They ate in silence, or at least they did after Cathy had finished her breakfast and toddled outside with Maria to play with her puppy. It was an easy, companionable silence. When the dishes had been cleared away and loaded into the dishwasher, they sat back down at the table, sharing sections of the newspaper, drinking their coffee.

At last Blade set the paper aside. "Jenny, I was

wondering if you had the time to spend the day with me."

Her heart leaped at that simple invitation as her eyes met the dazzling blue of his. He had the most beautiful eyes, she thought, too beautiful for a man, especially a man as rugged as Blade. They were such a startling, vivid color and fringed with thick dark brown lashes. There was a warmth in them that made her go hot all over.

"I haven't been able to get my old motorcycle started, and even when I do, I want something more practical to drive. So I've decided to go into Austin and buy a truck. I was hoping you'd go with me. We've been in-laws for ten years, and I don't think we've ever really talked. Maybe it's about time we did."

This from Blade Taylor, whom everyone said had no use for small talk with women? Blade, who used women for only one thing? She knew the truth of that, for hadn't he used her, too, that once? The shameful thing was that she hadn't minded.

She was as thrilled as a child, but she fought to keep her excitement out of her voice. She knew she should say no, feeling about him as she did, but of course she didn't.

"Why, Blade, I'd love to."

They had a wonderful time in Austin. Blade purchased a Ford Bronco after an hour's haggling with an obnoxious salesman, and the truck was to be delivered to the resort the next day. Blade bought some new clothes in a men's store, and it made Jenny feel all funny inside when she saw how handsome he was in everything he put on. He was so lean and virile, and the years had intensified his sultry sex appeal.

Jenny had packed sandwiches and a quilt, and on their way back to Zachery Falls they drove out toward South

Lamar to eat in Zilker Park on the high, grass-covered bank beside the Colorado River. In the park, sunshine filtered through the thick leaves overhead and sparkled on the water. Lovers wrapped in each other's arms lay on blankets beneath trees. Children were paddle-boating amidst a swarm of ducks. Couples canoed on the dark green river, their paddles barely stirring the languid water. A few hardy swimmers were doing laps down the length of Barton Springs, but the water was too cold for most, fed as it was by underground springs. The natural limestone pool was icy even on the hottest summer days.

When they finished with their picnic, Blade and Jenny lay beside each other, watching the clouds float by overhead.

"It was sweet of you to come with me today," Blade said. "I really appreciate it. You really gave that Ford guy a hard time at the end." He chuckled, remembering the way she'd stormed at the little man for the outrageous promises he'd made, demanding that he put them in writing.

"I just didn't like the way he was trying to take advantage of you."

"You always were one to fight other people's battles. I guess that comes from being a preacher's daughter." He smiled at her, but a trace of his old cynicism had crept into his tone. "But then, I wouldn't know much about that, would I? I'd always had too many battles of my own to fight to ever have the time to defend someone else. Sweet, sweet Jenny. We're about as different as two people can be." There was something almost angry in his voice when he said that.

Jenny hadn't come with him because she was sweet or noble, and as the day had passed, her reason for going along had preyed heavily on her mind. Sometimes she thought she was every bit as bad as he. Every time she looked at him, a flutter of excitement swept over her. Right now her eyes were tracing the broadness of his shoulders, the contours of his chest and stomach, the lines of his narrow waist—and her thoughts were not those of a lady.

She was marveling at the animal magnificence of his male body. This longing to touch him and for him to touch her was a new kind of torment. It had never been like this when she was with Dean, and she was at a loss to understand the terrible power of her feelings for Blade. She knew she should be thankful for this new friendliness with him, but she felt strangely restless. The devil within her was remembering the old, smoldering Blade, and it was difficult, so difficult, to feel thankful for mere friendliness when what she really wanted was something much different.

Suddenly she almost wished she were Susan Harper. She knew Blade would be different with Susan. He wouldn't lay here plucking at blades of grass and watching the clouds float by with his handsome face so cool and impassive. He would pull her beneath him, and he would kiss her with hot, possessive lips, and she would kiss him back, without shame. He would suggest a motel room, and she would say yes without a shadow of guilt.

Jenny felt warm suddenly, despite the cool spring air, at the mere thought of Blade's lips searing her flesh, at the thought of what he would do to her in the privacy of a motel room. She remembered how he'd kissed her before, how his mouth had kissed her everywhere, in secret, shamefully intimate places, learning her with his mouth as Dean never had.

It was wicked, the way she remembered it all so clearly. Because Blade was so near, and she could feel the warmth of him and catch the scent of him, the memory of that long-ago afternoon when he had made love to her came back to her with startling, poignant force. And all the time she lay remembering the wild, shameful glory of his loving, Blade went on infuriatingly plucking those blades of grass, deliberately ignoring her.

Jenny remembered how he had kissed her, his mouth hard and demanding until she'd opened her lips and accepted his tongue. Slowly, he had taught her the lure of passion, the song of the siren, with those long, wanton kisses on that drowsy spring afternoon when he'd awakened her innocent, untutored body to the splendor it had been designed for.

He'd undressed her and kissed every bit of bare feminine flesh he exposed, telling her how beautiful she was, exciting her as much with his words as with his lips. His hands had moved over her so gently that she'd marveled at the tenderness of the wild, untamed Blade Taylor.

How could he touch a woman thus, so that she shivered from the mere brush of a calloused fingertip? His lips had traveled to all the places his hands explored, trailing along the velvet skin of her throat, his mouth nibbling lower to the rounded tops of her breasts, and drifting lower still, pushing her hands aside and murmuring softly, "Leave me be, Jenny. There's no shame in being a woman. You're so beautiful." And she'd let him, and gloried in the letting.

Thinking of him and the way he'd loved her once, Jenny fell asleep beside Blade. The air was cool, and he smiled down at her beautiful, tranquil face. She was so innocently trusting. He removed his suede jacket and covered her slim shoulders with it.

In her sleep she murmured his name with a tenderness

that startled him, and she moved closer to him, seeking the warmth of his body as she cuddled more closely against him, pressing her breasts and hips to him, draping her arm over his waist.

Lord, why had she done that? How was a man to stay sane when he was inflamed by her merest gesture? He groaned inwardly when he felt the button-tips of her nipples through her sweater. His body hardened, but he didn't move away for fear of awakening her.

He couldn't resist caressing her, removing the pins from her hair and letting it fall across his arm where it gleamed in the sun like rich dark chocolate. He buried his face in the soft-smelling thickness even though it was a special kind of torture to do so. He moved his hand along her back, tracing the slim, soft line of her body down to the swelling of her hips. When she stirred, and he thought she might awaken, he let his hand fall away. He looked at her, savoring the beauty of her, the nearness of her.

They lay in each other's arms, and at last Blade fell asleep too, with his arms wrapped tightly around the woman he loved.

4

The kiddie train, loaded with laughing, squealing youngsters, whistled as it chugged past on its track near the tree in Zilker Park where Jenny and Blade lay, startling them. They awoke tangled in each other's arms and legs. Jenny was amazed that her hair had come loose from its knot and spilled in brown waves over Blade's shoulders. Several buttons on her red sweater had come undone again, and the shadowy indentation between her breasts was exposed.

What must he think? She flushed and felt embarrassed as she sat up, hastily pulling her body from his. Everywhere he touched her his skin scorched hers, filling her with wanton, pleasurable sensations that were wrong, under the circumstances.

She couldn't look at him as her fingers fumbled with the buttons of her sweater, and he read in her embarrassment disgust at having awakened and found herself in his arms.

Nothing had changed, he thought bitterly, the easiness he'd felt toward her suddenly leaving him. She was just like all the other nice women in Zachery Falls, who still thought he was filth and that they were too good to be touched by dirt like Blade Taylor. His stomach tightened with that old angry feeling he thought he'd put behind him when he'd left Zachery Falls ten years ago, and he jumped to his feet, his face so cold and dark that it made her want to cry as he began gathering their picnic things and throwing them into the basket.

They rode back to Zachery Falls in silence, each of them locked in their own private misery, yet each acutely conscious of the other. The brown hills whipped by as Blade drove, but neither saw them. He stopped only once, to buy a package of cigarettes at a drive-in grocery. She stayed in the jeep and chewed a fingernail until it was ragged and ugly and bleeding.

Blade had told her that he was trying to quit smoking, and the fact that he smoked now told her how angry he was. She stared at his face, trying to understand, but his chiseled features were as unreadable as a carved statue's. This was the inexplicably volatile Blade she remembered from the past, and she was at a loss to know what she had done to infuriate him.

Neither of them spoke until Blade roared past the entrance to Woodlands Hideaway without turning in.

Then, in a feeble voice she dared. "Blade, that was—"

"We're not going home just yet," he said, his voice low with suppressed anger.

"But why? Where are you taking me?"

"We have an appointment at Mike Kilpatrick's."

"On Saturday?"

"Mike told me he'd be in his office all afternoon, catching up on some work."

"But you didn't say anything about an appointment and neither did Mike."

"I asked him not to."

"You did what? Blade, what is going on? What's the matter with you?"

"You'll find out. Kilpatrick is being handsomely paid to explain all the legalities to you."

"But why won't you tell me yourself?"

"Because I don't feel like talking at the moment, if you don't mind."

She did mind, but he didn't say another word for the rest of the drive.

Once they alighted from the jeep they had to walk up a ramp and across a sidewalk to get to the law offices. Blade's face was still dark with the anger that ate at him on the inside and made him look fierce and dangerous on the outside. On their way to Mike's they passed several people they both knew. Katey Scudder stared at Blade with wide eyes and scarcely spoke to Jenny. Margaret Harris drew herself up haughtily and wouldn't even look at either of them. No one had ever cut Jenny dead in Zachery Falls before, but that was how they had always treated Blade.

Jenny saw that Blade's mouth was twisted in an even tighter line than before. He was walking so fast that she had to run to keep up with him, and she realized that he was not as indifferent to people disliking him as he had always pretended. All his old anger toward everyone had been a defense. Suddenly Jenny was furious that they felt they could treat him like that. How could they so self-righteously treat another human being as though he were dirt? Blade wasn't trash. He hadn't ever been. He'd just been a poor boy who was unfortunate enough to have been born to abusive parents—and the townspeople had abused him as well. He'd always deserved better. No wonder he'd acted so tough when he'd been younger.

It rubbed Blade's nerves raw when Mike came forward and took Jenny's hand in his as if it were his right and kissed her lightly on the cheek. He hated the way she accepted Kilpatrick's affection with a smile instead of flushing darkly as she had when she'd awakened in his own arms all mussed and deliciously sexy-looking. How he had wanted her then, before he'd realized what her feelings were. Then he'd gotten so angry he'd felt like smashing everything in sight. It was hell wanting someone who didn't want you.

Mike leaned across his desk and nervously handed a crisp set of legal papers to Jenny.

"But this is Caleb's will, and the papers for incorporating the resort. Why . . ." Jenny began.

"I'm giving you these papers so that you can read them at your leisure," Mike said slowly. "But if you'd like I'll briefly summarize the more pertinent facts for you. I've always felt that you should have known them, anyway."

What in heaven's name was going on? Why had Blade brought her here? And what did he have to do with any of the legalities involving the resort?

Blade sat silently beside her, his long legs crossed negligently as he leaned back and lit a cigarette. Even so, there was a tension in him, in Mike, and in the room.

"I don't understand the meaning of Blade's presence. Why do you feel it necessary to explain something involving my property in front of Blade?"

Mike and Blade looked at one another for a long, uncomfortable moment, but neither spoke. At last Mike began, and it was obvious he dreaded saying what he had to say.

"For one thing, Jenny, the property isn't just yours."

"What?"

"It belongs to Blade, too. Eight years ago Caleb left half of his estate, including half the ranch, to Blade. When Dean and I drew up the incorporation papers, Blade was a full partner."

"That can't be true."

"It is. I wanted to tell you when Dean died. The information was recorded in several legal documents that are in your possession."

"I never read them."

"I knew you didn't, and I tried to persuade Blade to tell you about it himself. Blade said he didn't want to upset you at the time. He said you had enough to make you unhappy without any additional problems. Earlier, both Blade and Dean had told me not to inform you about this unless it became absolutely necessary, and when Dean died, I thought it was necessary that you be told. But Blade insisted on sticking to the old promise he'd made Dean."

"What promise?"

"When Dean built the resort, he and Blade made a deal. Dean would manage the ranch and resort and send Blade's share of the profits to him. Blade promised he would never interfere unless he felt that he needed to. Unfortunately, Jenny, he feels that time has come. The loans that I've advanced you to keep Woodlands Hideaway afloat without the sale of acreage this last year have come from Blade. He's concerned about the management of Woodlands Hideaway. He's come home to take over.''

Jenny went white with shock, and she stared hard at both men, feeling bitterly confused. Dean had deliberately withheld this very vital piece of information from her, and Mike had known all along. For the two years since Dean's death, Mike had known, and still he hadn't told her that Blade owned half the ranch.

She was furious at both of them. They had treated her like a child.

She thought of how foolishly she'd behaved since Blade's return. She'd longed to see Blade even though she'd been afraid to. And when he'd moved in at the ranch she'd stupidly jumped to the conclusion that he must have cared in some way about Cathy and herself.

But Blade hadn't come back to live at the ranch out of any feelings for Caleb or Dean or for herself. He'd come back because of money. For ten years he'd stayed away, and as long as the ranch had remained profitable, it was obvious that he'd never had the slightest intention of returning. Doubtless he preferred the crude sports the townspeople accused him of—drinking and womanizing. He had no interest in working the ranch or running the resort as long as there was someone else to do it for him. At that moment, Jenny was mad enough to believe anything of him.

Blade was after money. That was the worst thing of all. All day she'd been so thrilled to be with him. Remembering the way she'd lain beside him in the park dreaming of the time he'd made love to her made her feel like a lovesick idiot. Why had she thought he might have cared about her? Why had she so stupidly allowed herself to idealize his motives?

Too, she'd behaved like a fool on the road this morning, crying all over him about her unhappiness. That feeling of closeness had been without foundation. What did he care? He was after the money, that was all.

She was madder at herself than she was at anyone else, but of course it was much more satisfying to vent her fury on Blade. "What makes you think you can run Woodlands Hideaway any better than I can, or that I'll let you?" She lashed out at him.

"I can hardly do worse." Blade's blue gaze was cool and steady as he regarded her. "As I see it, it's either run it better or sell out. At the debt we're carrying, we can't afford to continue with the monthly losses we've been sustaining. I've done some research and I've decided to hire a resort management company I'm favorably impressed with, Nichols Inc. I've met with Bob Nichols in Tennessee, and he's turned around resorts that have been in worse shape than Woodlands Hideaway. He's very enthusiastic about bringing his team out."

"You decided to hire this Bob Nichols without even consulting me?"

"That's right."

"And what if I'm against it?"

"You don't have any choice. I've got more money riding on Woodlands Hideaway than you do. In the last fourteen months you've accepted more than $100,000 from me in loans to keep the resort afloat. If you read the notes you signed, you'll understand the power I now have, power that you have given me."

"I can't believe that you—"

"Believe it. Jenny, you're a careless businesswoman. You have only yourself to blame if any of this comes as a surprise to you."

"Blade Taylor, you've always been hard. Maybe

everybody in Zachery Falls was right about you all along," she cried, knowing that she was being unfair, but too angry to care.

He shrugged, but the dark look that she hated was there on his face. "Maybe." Then he got up and turned to stalk out the door.

"Blade, I can't believe you're going to walk roughshod over me like this."

"If that's what you want to call it, you can believe it. As I see it, all I've done is hire a professional with twenty years of experience in the business. Nichols owns hotels of his own. He knows what he's doing, and you obviously don't. Unlike you, I'm willing to admit that I don't either, though I have every intention of learning. If you care to join me, you're welcome to come along for the ride. If not—" He hesitated, and the faintest hint of the devilish smile she found so disarming when they weren't angry at one another curved his sensual mouth. Only now, in her anger, she thought it derisive. "If not, I guess you could always stay home and take up a hobby. Why don't you give thumb-painting a try? From what I hear, a lot of people around Zachery Falls feel that that wouldn't be such a bad idea."

At that last she went red with fury. She started to say something, but all she could do was stutter crazily.

Blade swung the door open and walked out of the office just as Mike pulled Jenny into his arms and began to speak soothingly to her. But Blade had seen Kilpatrick embrace Jenny, and the knowledge that he was leaving them alone together burned through him as painfully as a tongue of fire as he strode down the long hall to the front of the building.

That old feeling of being shut out that he'd always had whenever he'd seen Dean and Jenny together was upon him, and he knew he had to get out of Zachery Falls fast before he did something he would regret.

For two days and two nights Blade did not return to the ranch. Jenny told herself that she was furious at him, that she hated him for the way he had so callously treated her, that she was indifferent to where he was and what he was doing. She accepted delivery on his Ford Bronco when it arrived only because it would have been spiteful not to. She worked at the resort as she always had, not mentioning to the employees that there were soon to be massive changes in management.

Despite her determination to be indifferent to Blade, every time she returned to the house from her office she couldn't help looking over at the garage to see if the Bronco was where she had left it, or to see if a light was on in his apartment. She told herself when she did these things that it was only human to be curious. It wasn't that she really cared.

Liar, a wiser voice whispered.

On the third night of his absence she was roused from her sleep by a loud series of noises outside. Heidi and her pup were barking, and something heavy seemed to be thudding upon the ground in the backyard.

Throwing on her robe, she crept to the back door and looked out. The light was on in Blade's apartment. Then she saw the shadow of a man by the doghouse. He was hacking clumsily at something on the ground, and then he stopped, leaning heavily on a hoe. She heard Heidi's whine and that of her pup and then the low croon of Blade's voice as he bent to pet the dogs.

She threw open the door and the moonlight slanted down upon her, illuminating the shape of her body through her thin negligee and peignoir.

"Jenny, what the hell do you think you're doing,

coming out here like that?" Blade muttered, his eyes moving over her.

"Maybe I should ask you the same thing," she replied undaunted, stepping onto the porch.

He was roughing Heidi behind her shaggy ear the way she liked to be petted. How was it that Blade Taylor knew so much about touching animals and women the way they enjoyed being touched? It was crazy how happy she felt that he was back.

"I heard the dogs carrying on, and I came over to see what the matter was," he explained.

His voice sounded funny, slurred. Uneasily she wondered if he'd been drinking.

"And?" she asked coolly.

"Just a little old rattlesnake."

"Just! In my backyard?" Horrified, Jenny rushed down the steps to investigate the inert coil beside the doghouse. Her nightclothes fluttered against her body, outlining the shape of her breasts, the slimness of her waist, and the length of her legs.

"My aim wasn't too good. I'm afraid I hacked up a few of your flowers before I killed him."

"Oh, I don't care!" she began passionately—then she smelled the liquor on his breath. "Blade, you've been drinking."

"It's true I haven't been in Sunday School. But then I'm afraid I've never laid claim to being the gentleman of your dreams. I'm not a Kilpatrick or a Dean." He laughed softly, and the rich sound of it in the darkness made her feel oddly excited.

"That's nothing to be so proud of."

"Who said I was proud of it?"

"Where have you been? With Susan Harper?" What had made her ask that last?

"You've got Susan on the brain, girl." He stepped closer, and there was that aura of wild danger about him that she remembered so well. His bold eyes raked her up and down, and she realized she should never have come out in the darkness with him. "As a matter of fact, I've been in Tennessee, meeting with Bob Nichols. He came back to Zachery with me, so we can begin work right away."

"Oh."

"It's plain to see you still think the worst of me, like everybody else in Zachery Falls. Everyone thinks that all I want is an easy woman and something to drink. Well maybe it's about time I lived up to your expectations. Or lived down to them, as the case may be. There can be fun in that kind of living, Jenny. Maybe it's time you learned that there's a hell of a lot more to life than church socials." Again there was that soft male laugh as he came toward her, still looking her up and down with hot eyes. "Don't you know it's dangerous to come out in the dark alone with a man like me when I'm half drunk and feeling wild?"

Involuntarily she backed toward the house. But despite her fear, she felt drawn to him. She felt like moving into his arms, instead of away from them. She wanted to be crushed against the hard length of him, to feel her mouth consumed by the heat of his.

She didn't know that her face had gone soft with desire.

"Jenny," he rasped, "you'd better go back into the house before it's too late."

Oh, would he never learn that she was as wicked as he? Perhaps that was at the bottom of this craving she had. Perhaps, just perhaps, it was time she taught him.

She didn't budge an inch, fascinated as she was by that untamed aura of maleness that clung to him, yearning for the magic of his touch. She stood looking at him with her heart in her eyes.

"Girl, you don't know what you're doing."

Oh, she knew.

"You're beautiful," he breathed in a voice that was hoarse and strange.

"Blade," she said shakily as his arms slid around her beneath the filmy robe to caress the bare warmth of her flesh. His languid stroking sent shivers through her, and she felt as if there were a dizzying hollow in the pit of her stomach. "Oh, Blade."

The stars were brilliant in the ink-black sky, and the cool night air was fragrant with the scent of wild flowers.

He could scarcely believe that she'd come to him like this. A wild joy flowed through him, and his hands tightened around her slim waist. He lifted her up and twirled her around in the sweet darkness. Her hair came loose and swirled down against his face. Her nightclothes floated like gossamer veils. She was laughing, and so was he.

Very slowly, he brought her back down to earth, letting the lithe firmness of her body slide erotically against his so that she could not help but learn the state of his arousal.

She stared at him, feeling suddenly shy and awkward, not being as experienced in these things as he. Her uncertainty grew, and she tried to pull away, wanting to run from the danger of him. But he held her fast, his mouth seeking hers.

He kissed her long and deeply, his tongue invading her mouth, his male body pressing close. His hands caressed her breasts as he molded her against him. When he released her at last, she stumbled backward, looking at him. In the moonlight his face was dark with passion, and his blue eyes held a wild glitter.

He was a stranger to her.

"Blade, I shouldn't. We shouldn't."

"Oh, but we should."

"No!" She took a step backward.

He didn't come after her because he knew that she would run if he did. He could easily take her by force. But he didn't think he'd have to.

"What a tease you are, Jenny Zachery," he said, but there was no anger in his voice. "To come out here like this and tempt me from the path of virtue—not that I've ever been one who minded being tempted from that path. And then when I'm all hot and bothered, you pull the temptation away." His low chuckle mocked himself as well as her. "You know, sometimes I think you're not as different from the Susan Harpers of the world as you like to pretend." At her look of shock, he said, "And that's not such a bad thing, either."

"I'm afraid, Blade."

"Why should you be afraid of being a woman?"

"I don't know. I guess I've always been afraid—of being *me*," she admitted.

"Maybe it's time you stopped."

"Dean—"

Dean! Always Dean! Blade didn't think he could stand it if she talked about Dean at that moment. Was he always to be there, between them, even when he was dead?

"I don't want to hear about how you love Dean, damn it," he growled, reaching for her.

The anger she saw in him reminded her of her fear,

and she ran toward the house, eluding him, stumbling up
the stairs. He caught her around the waist just before she
reached the door and pulled her fiercely against himself.
His mouth came down on hers hard, frightening in its
demand. He pushed her back against the wall, imprisoning her with his body, and he kissed her again and again
in a series of drugging kisses that left her limp and weak
and clinging to him. Hot tremors of exquisite longing
traced through her.

"Maria's inside, asleep in the house," she warned
when at last he released her lips so that his mouth could
nuzzle the softness of her throat. "I'll scream—"

"There won't be any screaming tonight, Jenny, girl.
Only loving," he murmured with a sexy chuckle. Then
his mouth smothered the cry she would have uttered, so
that it became no more than a helpless gurgle in her
throat.

His hands moved through her hair, caressing the
tumbling masses that fell about her shoulders.

"Jenny . . . Jenny. My God, Jenny, you're so beautiful, and I've wanted you so badly, so long, I thought I'd
die with the wanting." His eyes were smoldering with
passion as he lifted her into his arms, carrying her
effortlessly down the stairs and across the backyard
toward his apartment. He was panting slightly when he
reached the top of the stairs and kicked his bedroom
door open with his boot.

Inside the small, immaculate room he carried her to
the bed and laid her upon it, following her down. He
kissed her, and his hands moved over her body in a slow,
expert way that inflamed her every nerve ending. She
was thoroughly, breathlessly aroused when he finally
loosened the ribbons that fastened her robe and slid it
from her shoulders.

The lamp near the desk was on, and she said faintly, "Blade, the light. Turn it off."

"I want to see you."

"But—"

"I think you're beautiful. There's nothing to be ashamed of."

Dean had always made love to her in the darkness because of her shyness, and he'd never seemed to mind.

Blade removed her nightgown, and then he buried his lips against her navel, kissing her there with his tongue until wavelets of desire coursed through her everywhere from that erogenous spot. She placed her hands in his golden hair and held him close. It seemed that she'd always wanted this, as far back as she could remember. Only she'd never, never wanted to admit it.

At last he stood up and she watched, fascinated, as he undressed. Bronzed fingers started at the bottom of his blue shirt and unfastened the buttons one by one. He stripped off his shirt, and she marveled at the play of tanned muscles as he leaned over and hung the garment over the back of a chair. Slowly his fingers undid his belt buckle, and he slid his jeans off. In another moment he was naked. He looked like a Greek god. He was so beautiful, and she was wantonly thrilled that he was so obviously virile and all male, and so terribly, magnificently in need of a woman. She wanted to touch him there, but she felt afraid and shy at the same time.

When he came to her again his hands were shaking, so powerful was his desire. He was trembling all over. He lay on top of her, his body molded to her soft length, and he kissed her lips in that gentle and yet passionate way that could stir her soul.

Just as his hands were exploring Jenny, learning her readiness, the screen door of the ranch house slammed shut directly beneath them. The porch light flared, and Maria's anxious voice floated to them in the darkness. The thrilling sensations evoked within Jenny by Blade's touch were abruptly shattered.

"Mrs. Zachery!" came Maria's insistent cry.

They froze in one another's arms, each of them listening, Blade in frustration and Jenny in horror. They heard the sound of Maria's house slippers shuffling along the porch. Jenny stared out the window and watched the bobbing wand of light as the woman searched the darkness. Then Maria disappeared around the back of the house. Soon she would come to the garage, and perhaps she would even come upstairs.

"Blade, I can't let her find me like this with you," Jenny began desperately as she groped for her night-gown and robe.

"No, of course not."

His voice was low and cynical, and it hurt her some-how. His hands loosened upon her soft, warm body, and though she felt empty and lost, she left him. He made no move to stop her as she hastily dressed.

"I—I hope you can understand," Jenny said, but-toning her robe.

"Oh, I understand."

His face was dark and mocking, and Jenny thought that his broad grin was every bit as hateful as his cynical tone. He began to laugh softly.

"No, you don't," she said miserably and then she ran out the door into the sheltering darkness.

As she entered the backyard she called quietly to her maid. "You're making enough noise to wake the dead, Maria."

"So there you are." The dark eyes in the brown face were speculative.

"There was a rattlesnake in the backyard. I was going to put the hoe in the garage."

"Oh." Maria was only half-believing, perhaps because the hoe was still leaning against the doghouse.

"You can see for yourself. Look on the ground beside the doghouse," Jenny said coldly as she swept past the other woman and went inside.

When she was safely inside her bedroom, Jenny's thoughts returned to Blade. She wondered what he was thinking. He hadn't liked her leaving him.

But she had liked it no better than he. She'd wanted him for so long. Even now her blood ran hot at the thought of his touch, his kisses. His passion had inflamed all the feelings that had lain dormant within her, intensifying them. The shattering fulfillment she'd known only once had been tantalizingly within reach only minutes ago. Now all that was lost to her, and it was more painful than ever that she had to sleep in her cold bed where she felt so achingly alone.

Blade couldn't sleep either. Instead, he dressed and stepped out into the darkness. For a long time he stood in the shadows of an oak tree, watching the house, wanting Jenny so much that it hurt. Heidi came to him to have her ears scratched.

Blade stooped and petted the dog. "At least you're getting what you want, girl," he said gently. He stared at Jenny's darkened window again.

It was no use wanting what he couldn't have, he told himself harshly.

Jenny wanted him the same way she'd wanted him when she was a girl, and she was ashamed of the wanting. She didn't want anyone to know how she felt. Not that he blamed her.

But he didn't like it, either, and the hurt she'd inflicted swelled into a fierce, dark anger against her. If it hadn't been for his desire to do right by Caleb and his granddaughter, Blade would have left Zachery Falls forever that night. Instead, he decided to go to the resort bar and see if Bob Nichols was still there.

5

When Jenny awoke, she felt just as exhausted as she had when she'd gone to bed. She was numb with the pain of wanting and denying that she wanted. If only she'd had the courage to give herself to Blade. But he hadn't really wanted her. He'd only been drinking, and she'd been available. She should be glad that Maria had come outside and saved her from herself.

But she wasn't glad, and that was wrong. But then, everything she was thinking and doing these days was wrong. What was happening to her? To her morals? To her sense of values?

It was wrong for her to take such pleasure in the arms of a man when love words had never been spoken between them, and probably never would be. When, indeed, she knew that Blade didn't love her, not the way Dean had loved her, in the noble, respectable, sensible way that led to a conventional marriage and two lives joined together. When she even doubted that he could really love a woman, let alone marry one and live respectably. But Blade needed her in a way that Dean never had, and somehow, although it was against everything she believed in to yearn to sleep with a man she wasn't married to, she was excited by the way Blade wanted her with that all-consuming passion. It was exciting to think of him desiring her and not just respecting her for all her virtuous qualities, the way everyone else did.

But then, why *would* he respect her, knowing her in the way that he did? A tiny voice nagged at her. What would everyone else think if they learned the truth about her?

It was the hypocrite in Jenny who wanted everyone in Zachery Falls to go on thinking well of her; it was the hypocrite who had made her run from Blade's lovemaking at the first sound of Maria's voice. It would never, never do for the Widow Zachery to be found in bed with Blade Taylor. But the woman in Jenny yearned—and knew it was wrong to yearn.

The sunlight flooding Blade's room spilled its white brilliance into his face. He groaned as he grew aware of a terrible pain that seemed to split his head in two. He sat bolt upright, and the pain pounded through him more strongly than before.

"Damn, what the hell—" But the feeling was not all that unfamiliar, although in recent years he hadn't had cause to suffer from it often.

Blade remembered the whiskey he'd consumed in the resort bar with Bob Nichols; then he remembered Jenny, and the way her face had looked, beautiful and soft with desire.

Staring at his rumpled pillow, he buried his face in his hands. What had he almost done?

But he knew what he'd done, and as he dragged himself out of bed and walked toward the shower, he was swamped by the most terrible feelings of remorse he'd ever known. He'd almost taken what a woman like Jenny would never have willingly given him. He remembered how she'd run from him, how she'd tried to scream on the porch, how quickly she'd left him when she'd heard Maria, and those blurred memories made him feel worse.

He stepped into the shower, feeling queasy as he forced himself to endure the splintering chill of the water spraying down upon him. How would he ever face her? Like a coward, he knew that he couldn't, not right now. So he dressed hurriedly and went down to the restaurant to have breakfast with Bob Nichols.

From the house, Jenny heard Blade's Bronco on the road, and she rushed to the window only to see him drive away. Filled with a wrenching sadness, she watched until the plume of dust that had billowed behind the truck settled once more on the road.

Did he despise her now, for what she had done? She wanted to die of shame for letting him know how she wanted him, and also what a hypocrite she was, at the same time. But, of course, she could not. Cathy began to cry, and Jenny left the window to see what was the matter.

After breakfast Jenny dressed in a long-sleeved gray cotton dress that was as demure as a puritan's garb. She pinned her hair in a prim knot at the nape of her neck and stared at herself hard in the full-length mirror in her bedroom. There were no telltale ravages of passion evident upon her smooth alabaster skin. Satisfied, she left for her office.

Blade's Bronco was parked in front of the resort's lodge, but she didn't see him that morning, though she remained nervous and expectant in anticipation that she might. When she finished writing the innumerable promotion letters she went down to the restaurant for lunch. She was already inside the dining room when she heard the sound of Blade's laughter. There was no way she could bolt from the room like a startled goose flapping for cover, so, feeling mortified, she headed to a nearby table and sank down in a chair with her back to the place where Blade was sitting with several men. She gave her order to the waiter and tried to ignore the uneasiness she felt at being near Blade.

The carpet in the restaurant was thick and soft, so she didn't hear Blade's tread as he approached.

"Jenny—" Blade's soft, deep voice came to her from behind.

It was difficult to raise her eyes to his.

His face was dark and remote. There was a bleakness in his eyes that tugged at her heart. Suddenly she longed for the easiness that had been between them the day they'd gone to Austin. Had she lost even that because of last night?

"I was hoping you would join us. I'd like for you to meet Bob Nichols and the men he's brought with him from Tennessee," Blade said.

No words of tenderness. No indication that there had ever been anything between them. Jenny's stomach clenched into a knot as tightly wound as that of her hair. She wanted to cry, to nurse her hurt in private, but of course that was impossible under the circumstances. She couldn't very well refuse him, so she nodded mutely, wishing all the while that she could sink into the middle of the earth or some other place equally far removed from Blade Taylor.

She did not know of the pain that her silence and the dull unhappiness in her face brought him, nor of the control in him that prevented his going down on his knees and begging her forgiveness. Never had he loved her more than now, when he thought he'd lost even her friendly regard.

When his hand touched the back of her waist as he escorted her to his table, she was terribly aware of it, and she flinched away from his fingers. She didn't see the darkness that came to his eyes when he felt her reaction.

Bob Nichols was silver-haired and fatherly, a man well into his sixties. He reminded Jenny of Caleb, and she wondered if that was why Blade thought so highly of him. Throughout lunch his conversation was filled with practical suggestions for immediate changes and expenditures. He had a three-phase scheme for making the resort profitable. To her surprise, Jenny found that she felt only relief as she listened to Blade and the men talk. Her original resistance to the situation melted away as she listened to Bob's commonsense solutions to problems that had seemed to her insoluble. It seemed to her that Blade had lifted a horrendous burden from her shoulders by coming home and hiring Bob, and when she remembered the way she had treated him in Mike's office, she felt truly ashamed. She'd been so ignorant, so frightfully ignorant. She'd lashed out and said things she should never have said.

It pleased her when Bob complimented a few of the areas where she'd actually done the right things. To her astonishment, she realized that she was actually looking forward to all the changes that were going to be made. Of course, they would not be easily implemented. The staff would balk and want to cling to the old, comfortable ways. But as she left the table, she felt positive that they would at least make a start in setting things right.

In the week that followed, things did not improve between herself and Blade. He avoided her. During the days when she was in the office, he stayed away from that part of the resort. During the evenings he didn't come home until long after she had gone to bed. She would lie in bed, wondering where he was, torturing herself with visions of him in Susan's bed.

When he chanced upon her at the lodge or anywhere else in the resort, he was stiff and uncomfortable in her presence. He would quickly find some excuse to leave and see to something else if it became obvious that she had to stay where he was for a while. She was relieved when he left because his coldness hurt her so.

It killed her, the way he wanted nothing to do with her, the way he stayed away as if he couldn't stand the sight of her. Nevertheless, every night she cried herself to sleep after she heard his truck drive up and his footsteps on the stairs.

How she longed for him to come home earlier, to walk up to the front porch, knock on the door, invite himself inside. She envisioned him lifting Cathy high above his shoulders while she squealed with delight. Then later, when the child was content to play by herself, Jenny imagined Blade coming close and folding her in his arms and holding her tightly against him. They would laugh and talk quietly and share things, the special secret things that only lovers share. All the pain that had been locked within her for so long would dissolve and flow out of her, and she would love and be loved.

But, of course, Blade was not that sort of man, and he did none of those things. He went on avoiding her, and she went on longing for him, her spirit crushed by her secret sorrow. Hopelessly she wondered if time would ease the hurt so that she could learn to stand his indifference. All she knew was that when Blade Taylor had come home, he'd turned her world upside down, and she no longer knew how to live.

Blade worked hard in the month that followed, harder than Jenny, harder than Bob Nichols, harder than anyone at Woodlands Hideaway. Jenny watched him, admiring the way he worked undaunted despite the innumerable setbacks and all the complexities he had yet to learn about the business.

He took inventories of every guest room and every town house in the hotel rental pool. He read ten years' worth of income tax returns, poured over account books, went through every piece of paper in every filing cabinet, spent long hours talking to the employees and to the town house owners.

She couldn't have known that it was his longing for her that drove him to work until he could collapse in bed in a state of exhaustion. Even when he didn't get to bed until midnight and he'd been up since dawn, he sometimes lay awake, haunted by her. Every time he chanced upon her at the resort he drank in the startling beauty of her. He could not stop himself from mentally stripping the clothes from her body and remembering the voluptuous femininity that had so aroused him, even when these visions brought him sharp pain. Yet he was careful to hide his feelings, for her sake, reminding himself that Kilpatrick and Dean were the sort of men she could want without shame.

For Jenny the days passed listlessly, hopelessly.

One bright Friday morning in May, Carol Thompson, the head of housekeeping, came into Jenny's office with the news that two television sets had been stolen from Town House 34. Jenny pulled out the file on the town house only to discover that those sets were brand new; only a month before, two sets had been stolen from that very same town house. Jenny was about to pick up the phone and call the owner when she decided to go to Blade first.

His secretary ushered her into his office and then left, closing the door behind her. They were alone. Blade was on the phone, but he nodded to Jenny to sit down.

Her heart tripped with an odd little pang at the sight of him. This was the first time in over a month that they'd been alone together. She relished the chance to look at him. His skin was browner from the hot Texas sun; the golden hair that tumbled over his brow so rakishly had grown longer. She was achingly aware of the size of him, of the broadness of his shoulders, and of his hard muscular body, as well as of the deep yearning that lay within her to go into his arms and become a part of him.

He was so handsome. She knew he could have any woman he wanted, even one of those in town who professed to despise him. Jenny had to fight against the sickening sensation of jealousy as she wondered for the millionth time about the women he must surely be seeing.

"What is it, Jenny?" Blade asked at last after he'd hung up the phone. His vivid eyes met hers with a little of their old intensity. She was more aware than ever of his animal magnetism, and she flushed at the wanton thoughts that went through her head.

"I hate to bother you with this," she began hesitantly.

"Don't you know by now that you're never a bother?" he said, his tone almost as easy as it had been before that night of passion and hypocrisy.

"Blade, two more television sets have been taken out of Town House 34."

"Two more? Did you know that we've lost eighteen color sets from the town houses alone in the last two months?"

"I knew we'd lost some, but until Carol came to my office this morning—"

"Some!" Blade rose from his chair, jamming his hands deep into his pockets, and went to stare out the window that overlooked the pool and the tennis courts. "The town house owners are up in arms, and I don't blame them. Those television sets cost nearly five hundred dollars apiece."

"But, Blade, there doesn't seem to be anything we can do." She spoke hesitantly.

He looked at her, his blue eyes sharp. "I think there is."

"What?"

"Wait and you'll see," he returned cryptically. Since she could think of no excuse to remain in his office, she got up to leave. He followed her. She was at the door when his voice stopped her.

"Jenny—"

She turned and her eyes met blue ones that were brilliant with an emotion she couldn't define. Her pulse thudded with sudden pleasure. Surely he couldn't look at her like that if he didn't feel something for her.

"I was wondering—" He hesitated.

"Yes, Blade?" She tilted her face inquiringly, scarcely daring to hope.

"I was wondering if you could help me with something."

"Of course."

"One of the employees can't make the resort hayride tonight, and we don't have anyone else to drive the tractor or host the dance. I offered to take his place, but I've never done it before. I was wondering if you would mind helping me."

It was only business. It wasn't as if he were asking her for a real date, as if he wanted to be with her for herself alone, but Jenny felt thrilled nevertheless. She blushed, radiant.

"Why, yes, Blade. I'd be happy to, that is if Maria doesn't have plans to go out." Jenny said that last just so she wouldn't sound too eager.

It was a perfect evening for a hayride. The sun was sinking in a haze of pink gold, and the full moon was yellow as it came up on the opposite horizon. The air smelled of sweet budding flowers and tart, fragrant juniper.

Adults and children clambered, laughing, into the wagon after Jenny collected their tickets and passed out their name tags. Though Blade had scarcely spoken to her since she'd arrived, his smile of greeting had left her as breathless and as excited as though she were a young girl with her first crush. Indeed, she felt young, giddily, delightfully young, as she'd never felt when she'd actually been young.

When the wagon was loaded and Jenny had finished listing the safety rules, she was about to take her place in the hay with the guests, but Blade came to her. She felt the light, possessive pressure of his fingers at her elbow, and her heart leaped at his touch.

"I need you to ride up front with me, Jenny, if you don't mind. To show me the way," he explained in that low voice that set off vibrations deep within her.

She nodded, feeling weak with joy at his invitation.

Odd, Blade saying that, when he'd grown up on Zachery Ranch, and still knew every inch of it better than any living human being. She was too thrilled to question him, however, too radiantly happy when he helped her up on the seat beside him to say anything that might cause him to change his mind.

They rode in silence, each wishing the other would speak, until at last Jenny did.

"This makes me remember how it was when we were kids," she said softly. "Do you remember Caleb always letting Dad bring the church youth group out here for our annual hayrides?"

Blade remembered only too well. He remembered how alone, how shut out he'd felt when he'd watched all the kids pile into the hay. He remembered the way they'd teased each other and acted silly, their manner so young and carefree in a way he'd never been young. Some secret part of him had longed to be one of them, however much he'd tried to deny it. Hell, sometimes Blade thought he'd been born grown up. Or was it just that Jamie's beating him and neglecting him had done that?

Blade said nothing, not wanting to remind Jenny of the chasm that had always separated them.

"We used to sing songs and kiss, and giggle about it all. Why is it that songs always sound the best when you're outside, when you're young and caught up in the excitement of what seems like an adventure?"

Blade didn't know quite what she was talking about, but he liked the sound of her voice in the darkness and the pleasant sensation of her nearness.

"Blade, how come you'd never go with us back then? Dad always begged you to, and remember that time I asked you, too? But you wouldn't come that night, either."

Blade remembered how she'd come up to the ranch house especially to ask him. That had been before he'd moved into the apartment above the garage. Jenny had always been nice to him. He'd been showering when he'd heard the door, and he'd answered it wearing only a pair of jeans. When he'd seen Jenny standing there in the soft light of the porch, looking so pretty in her dress of gingham and ruffles, his heart had seemed to stop and then start up again in a fierce rush of youthful, painful excitement. He'd been about to duck back inside after his shirt. It had seemed too intimate, too dangerous somehow, standing half dressed when they were alone at the house. But she'd called him back in that shy, sweet way of hers that he could never resist.

"Please don't go, Blade."

"I was only going after my shirt," he'd said gruffly.

She'd spoken softly. "I like you like that. I think you're beautiful, you know."

Then she'd turned red at her boldness, and that made her seem even prettier to him. And it made what she'd said even sexier, somehow. Imagine a girl like Jenny Wakefield liking to look at him and being scared of those feelings, but brave enough, nevertheless, to speak her mind. He'd noticed how she went on looking at him despite her shyness. He'd liked the feel of those hot green eyes too much, and it was that night that he'd first begun to think he couldn't live if he couldn't have her.

"I only came up to tell you all the kids are down at the barn, ready for the hayride," she said. "Won't you come, too? You never have, you know, and this is our senior year and your last chance."

"You should leave me alone, preacher's daughter." The thrill he felt at her asking him made his voice sound rough, and he had to make an effort to conceal his feelings. "Don't you know what everyone says about me?"

"I know. But I don't believe half of it."

"Maybe you should."

"Maybe." She batted her lashes in that shy way of hers that charmed him. "And maybe not. Maybe you're not half so tough and mean as everybody says. If you're so mean, Blade Taylor, why do you go out when it's freezing and help cows with their birthings? Why did you tend that sick calf day and night for three weeks straight, 'til Caleb made you stop because you got sick yourself? Why are you afraid to stand out here in front of me without your shirt? No, I don't think you're mean and tough. I think you're shy and scared. You're a coward, same as me."

"I'm no coward!" he'd yelled down at her through the screen, but inside he knew she was right. He was scared of not fitting in with people, of the other kids and what they said when his back was turned. And she was right about his shirt, too. He'd wanted it because it seemed safer somehow to be around her with the barrier of all his clothes between them, and he respected her more than any girl he knew. He was uncomfortable with her knowledge of him; it was an invasion of his inner self.

Without thinking, he'd shoved the screen door open angrily, and he'd stepped out onto the porch.

"You shouldn't have come up here, preacher's daughter," he said mockingly. "'Cause you're wrong about me. I'm not like your friends at the barn."

"I know."

Her voice was sweet and soft and sexy. Suddenly all his anger was gone and in its place was that powerful emotion he felt for her that was always just beneath the surface, the emotion he'd always fought to hide.

She didn't try to run when he pulled her into his arms and crushed her slim body between the porch pillar and his own young, muscular frame. She smelled of rose water and other delicious feminine fragrances, and he'd groaned as his need for her rose within him. It was hell being male and young and wanting so badly a girl who was innocent and virginal.

"This is crazy, you know, a guy like me wanting a girl like you. But I do. I always have."

He felt like a fool, pouring his heart out to her. He was as corny as any soap opera character. Tough Blade Taylor. He never said things like that to a girl.

But Jenny was different. She had always been so special to him.

He stared at her and was dazzled by her youthful beauty. Her pale skin was aglow, and the silken masses of her brown hair framed the loveliness of her face. She was exquisite, small and gracefully slender, with rounded, firm breasts that swelled temptingly against her dress. He felt them rise and fall slowly against his bare chest with her every breath. Oh, she was sweet, sweet torture, but he couldn't let her go.

His arms were around her narrow waist, and he lifted her from the porch floor, bringing her hard against his strong body. He bent his head and kissed her full on the lips. He explored her soft, surprised mouth without any hurry even though his entire body was suffused with surging desire.

He knew enough about women to know that Jenny, for all her innocence and purity, was more hotly responsive than any girl he'd ever kissed. Her lips were trembling beneath his. There was that magic of touching and being touched by the other between them, that rarity of bonding that exists between a man and the right woman.

"Open your mouth," he instructed.

She moaned, then obeyed so that his tongue could thrust deeply inside.

When one of his hands slid to her breast, she held herself very still, like a frightened fawn, and then ever so tentatively she leaned into the cup of his fingers as if she wanted the intimacy of his hands on her body more than she wanted anything. She was breathless from his kisses, from his holding and caressing her, and he felt her fingertips in his hair. He felt her other palm running wonderingly across the expanse of his broad shoulders. At last she pulled away, as if the touch of him was too exquisite to endure. Though his every instinct cried out to him to stop her, he loosened his hold.

"Oh, Blade, Blade—" She sighed, her sweet voice whispery and passionate, her green eyes darkly afire.

She did a strange thing then. She placed one of her small hands on either side of his face, framing it as if it were very dear to her, as if she truly loved him. Though it was a powerful eroticism, her caressing him like that with such tenderness, he did not kiss her again or press her close as he wanted to.

"Blade, if you're bad, then what am I? I shouldn't be here like this. I should hate it when you kiss me, loving Dean as I do. He's asked me to marry him as soon as we graduate, and I'm going to. But why do I keep thinking of you? Why does it make me feel so strange just to look at you? So you see, Blade Taylor, I know all about being bad, 'cause I'm just as bad as you."

She'd begun to cry then, just as Dean came around from the back of the house. Dean took one look at his shirtless brother and his girl friend in tears and caught the passionate undercurrents of the scene. Not understanding them, his mind leaped to the nastiest possible conclusion.

"Did he try to hurt you, Jenny? Or treat you like one of his girls?" Dean hollered. "Because if he did, I'll—"

Jenny instantly rallied and stepped between them. "No, of course not, Dean."

"It'd be just like him!"

"What the hell have you ever known about me, Dean Zachery?" Blade cried, stung by his brother's accusation, and by the strange jealousy that Dean's protective arms around Jenny provoked.

"It's all my fault, Dean," Jenny said quietly. "I came up here to invite him on the hayride, and he said—"

"What did you do a fool thing like that for?" Dean demanded, suddenly angry at Jenny. "Haven't I told you often enough what he's like?"

At that Blade jumped toward his brother with clenched fists, but before he reached him, Jenny's hand came up, touching his bare arm ever so lightly, her green eyes huge and pleading when they met his.

"Please, Blade, don't fight him. He's just mad, and so are you. I can't bear to be the cause of trouble between you."

Funny, how her soft plea had taken all the anger out of him. "All right," he replied gruffly, and without a word he'd gone back inside the house, though it hurt like hell, leaving her like that with Dean. Later, he imagined her buried deep in a pile of hay with Dean kissing her in all the soft, sweet places Blade had wanted to explore with his lips, and that had hurt even more.

Blade had gone out that night, but none of the girls he'd found and none of the wild things they'd done to pleasure him had made him forget the way a preacher's daughter had told him that she liked him without a shirt, that she liked him holding her and kissing her, and thought she was bad because she did.

It was then that his desire for her had started to consume him like the slow smoldering of a spark before it bursts into flame. He was that spark, ready to burst. It was then that he began to seek her out so that she would talk to him in her shy, sweet way, so he could feel the heat of her gaze as she watched him when she thought he didn't notice. Not long afterward she'd ridden over on horseback to Zachery Ranch, claiming that she was looking for Dean, though Blade was practically certain he'd heard Dean tell her over the phone he would be in Austin all that day.

Blade had offered to ride with her part of the way home across the Zachery land. Deliberately, he'd suggested that they stop to talk beneath the shade by Cypress Creek, and all too soon he'd taken her into his arms and kissed her in a slow, hot way that aroused them both and showed them the scorching power of the youthful desire that was between them.

They'd made love that afternoon, and she'd cried afterward, making him feel terrible for what he'd done. Maybe if she hadn't cried and acted so frightened and ashamed of herself, he wouldn't have felt so awful. But he'd felt ashamed, too. Imagine tough Blade Taylor's conscience hurting because he'd taken a girl who'd been as willing as any he'd ever had.

After that he'd stayed out of her way, hating himself for his monstrous selfishness, for taking her that way when she really loved Dean.

"You're very quiet tonight, Blade," Jenny said softly, bringing him back to the present, back to the roar of the tractor and the laughter and singing of the hotel guests in the haywagon that rumbled behind them, but most of all back to her gentle presence beside him.

"I was thinking back to when we were kids," was all he said.

Things hadn't changed. Not really. He wondered if they ever would.

Blade slanted a sidelong glance at Jenny. She seemed just as unreachable as ever, and his wanting her was still the same.

What in the hell was he going to do about it?

6

Blade drove on, and Jenny noted that not once did he ask her for directions as the tractor jolted down the road in the velvet, star-brightened darkness. When they reached the wide grassy spot by the creek where the barbecue cookout and dance were to be held, Jenny saw that, as always, lanterns had been hung in the low branches of the oaks above the wooden and concrete platform that was used as a dance floor. Resort workers were bustling around the barbecue pits. Long tables swathed in red-and-white-checkered tablecloths had been placed near the creek and bandstand. Almost immediately the band began to play familiar country and western music, and the guests began to sing along enthusiastically.

Blade helped Jenny down, and without a word to each other they went to work. Jenny gave directions to the guests, pointing the way to the rest rooms and the bar and to the tables of hors d'oeuvres.

As the party progressed, and Blade continued to avoid her, Jenny's spirits sank. It seemed to her that nothing had changed between them, that Blade hadn't wanted her with him tonight after all. She'd been foolish to hope.

It hurt the way all the female guests between the ages of eight and eighty flocked around Blade, but what hurt the most was the way he seemed to enjoy their attentions. He laughed and joked with every woman—every woman except her. At the moment he was dancing beneath the trees with a pretty girl named Louise, who couldn't have been a day over twenty. Her raven head rested dreamily on Blade's shoulder, and her eyes were closed.

Jenny shuddered with the painful throb of her jealousy and decided it was foolish and masochistic to watch them. She decided to try and find something to occupy herself. As she turned to go to the buffet line, she found herself facing Ross Jackson, a wealthy hotel guest from San Antonio. He was middle-aged and a little overweight, but oddly charismatic nonetheless.

He grinned broadly. "You're just the little lady I was looking for. Would you like to dance, Mrs. Zachery?"

Usually Jenny avoided dancing with the resort guests, but as she slanted her eyes toward the couple beneath the trees, the pain she felt at the sight made her say lightly, "Why, I'd like that, Ross, very much."

Ross was a big talker, and he continued to talk even while he danced.

"I'm mighty impressed with your resort, little lady. Mighty impressed. So impressed, in fact, that I'm very tempted to invest in a couple of lots and that town house that's up for resale."

"Why, thank you, Ross."

"That Blade Taylor seems to have a level head on his shoulders, despite what a few people say."

Jenny tensed at the mention of Blade and at the hint that he was being criticized in town. Would the gossiping about Blade never cease? When would people learn that he was just ordinary, like everybody else?

"He's very capable and very hardworking, and he always has been," Jenny said in Blade's defense. "No matter what people say."

"That's the way he struck me—but when I was in town that's not what I heard. Folks are mad about him popping up, claiming half of what's yours and your child's."

"It's none of their business, Ross," Jenny said grimly.

"You're mighty quick to defend him," Ross said perceptively. "Mighty quick. I wonder—"

"Don't! He's my brother-in-law! That's all. And my partner. I don't like the way people around here always talk about other people's business. Once they start on someone they never seem to stop. They've been talking about Blade since the day he was born."

"I guess that's the way with most small towns, in Texas, anyway. But, little lady, if I were you and I didn't like people talking, I'd at least make him move out of that garage apartment, and quick. People are talking about that, you know."

"What?"

Ross's expression was gentle. "Well, what would you expect in a town like this? They're talking about him living out there all alone with you."

Jenny flushed with anger, not at Ross, but at the thought of the malicious gossip going on behind her back. She was remembering the speculative glances she'd received of late. Until this moment she hadn't thought much about it.

Fortunately, the music ended. Jenny was so upset she couldn't have danced another step. In fact, she was so upset that she had to go off by herself for a minute before she could face people again.

When Ross left her she didn't return to the party. Instead, she walked along the path beside the creek until it meandered into a steep, wide bank near some smooth rocks. She sat down on a rock and stared unseeingly at the silvery water as it rippled in a glistening cascade over a manmade dam.

Why were people so cruel? Why did they want to think the worst of Blade, and now of her?

But it *was* true in a way, what they were saying, a tiny little voice whispered.

Not anymore. Not anymore. Blade hadn't even looked at her in weeks. And that was more painful and humiliating than anything. More painful even than the gossip.

In the darkness she didn't see Blade's careful approach. The gurgling of the creek and the whine of violins in the distance concealed the sound of his footsteps on the rocky path.

Blade's voice came to her, hushed and vibrant and achingly masculine.

"Jenny—"

Her heart began to pound jerkily. She hadn't wanted him to find her like this. Still, she couldn't stop herself from responding to his gentleness.

"Over here," she replied dully.

"You okay?"

"Sure."

"You don't sound it. Did Ross make a pass at you? Because if he did—"

"Don't be ridiculous. All he said was that he was impressed by what you've done here since you've come back. He's thinking of investing in a lot or two and a town house."

"Jenny, that's wonderful. I don't need to tell you how much we need the capital we'd realize from a sale like that."

Blade moved closer, and then she could see him in the moonlight. His hair was silver fire as it tumbled against his dark face. He was so tall, so magnificently lean and broad-shouldered. As always she felt excited just at being alone with him, and she ached for his arms to close around her, for his body to press into hers so that she could feel the warm, muscular power of him. But all he thought about these days was the resort and making money, she remembered with a flash of resentment. He avoided her and sought other women like Louise, the girl he'd been dancing with.

"Yes. It's just great," Jenny said flatly, turning away from him.

"What happened, then, to upset you?" Blade persisted.

"Would you just go away and leave me alone?"

"No."

His voice was right behind her now, and the sympathy in it made her heart rush.

His fingers closed gently upon her shoulders, and the thrill she felt at his touch was almost painful.

"Jenny—"

Why was it that just the way he said her name could make her feel so pleasantly warm, so sexily female?

"Girl, is it impossible for us to talk?"

"That's what they say about you, isn't it?" she lashed

out irrationally. "That you can't talk to a woman. That you can only use her in a physical way."

"Where in the hell is all this coming from?" he demanded, the first trace of anger entering his low tone.

"Just go back to the party."

"You're gonna tell me what's wrong because I'm not leaving 'til you do." His fingertips played with her hair, and she felt herself going as soft as mush at his nearness.

She whirled, angered at both herself and him for the ease of her responsiveness to him, angered still more when she remembered the way he'd danced with the other girl. "All right, since you insist. Ross said people in town were talking about you and me, about us living out here alone together. And I don't like it!"

He went white in the moonlight, his tanned face as pale and sickly as bleached bone, and that shuttered look that she hated was in his eyes.

"So that's it." His voice was no longer soft, but harsh and filled with anger. His fingers tightened on her arms. "Things never change, do they?"

"I don't suppose they do. Not around here, anyway," she replied in a low, dreary voice.

"It must be awful for you, your name being linked with mine. You told me the first night I came out here that you didn't want me living on the ranch because people would talk."

Had she said that? His voice sounded so odd, almost as though he were hurt. Had she hurt him by saying that? Did he care for her after all?

"Blade, sometimes I say things I don't mean."

"Or maybe you do mean them. Beneath the surface maybe you're just like everybody else in Zachery Falls, ready to think the worst of me, ready to think that I'm so depraved I can't keep my hands off a decent woman even if she happens to be my sister-in-law. Sometimes I think I'm a damned fool for coming back here and working my guts out to save the ranch for you and Cathy."

She turned to him in wonder, and her eyes met the glittering darkness of his.

"Blade, is that why you came back—to help me?"

"I thought you believed the gossip about me," he ground out fiercely as he dragged her into his arms, pulling her against his body. "That I don't do anything for anybody except myself, that I came back to take the ranch and maybe use you for a while in the bargain. The hell with them," he said bitterly. "The hell with everyone in Zachery Falls! I'm sick of them turning my life inside out and making me into what I'm not." His hands moved over her in angry possession. "You're mine. You've always been mine. They're right, you know, in a way. I came back because I wanted you. I came back to take what's always been mine. Maybe it's time I did."

The sensual curve of his mouth was cruel and terrifying as he bent closer.

"Blade, don't." She wanted him, but not like this, not when he was angry and determined to be deliberately hateful. She reached up to place her hand placatingly on his chest.

"Why the hell not?" He seized her hand in his and brought it roughly to his mouth, kissing her wrist with passionate anger until she trembled from the touch of his lips. She knew that he felt the leap of her pulse beneath his mouth. "And what would people say if they knew the whole truth?" he began, his velvet voice very male and cynical. "If they knew how you tempted me with your kisses and your wildness? If they knew how you teased me and then hid behind your damnable ladylike virtue and hypocrisy? If they knew that you wanted the man they all despise and that you were too cowardly to own up to the wanting?"

"Blade—"

"Shut up, Jenny. Maybe people are right after all. Maybe a man like me can't put things into words with a woman. Maybe a man like me has no use for talking at all, no use for anything but taking and using a woman the way she was made to be used. You're a woman, Jenny Zachery, for all your attempts to pretend otherwise. Maybe it's time I made you *my* woman."

Blade's arms crushed her slim body hard against his own. His mouth claimed hers at last with a kind of wild, desperate urgency. For a month he'd left her alone because he'd thought that was what she wanted, and he'd had no other women, though there had been plenty who had chased after him. What Jenny had said about hating to hear her name linked with his enraged him. He was filled with frustrated desire, filled with anger that he couldn't have her, that no matter what he did to please her she was determined to humble him. He kissed her again and again with hard, bruising lips, not caring if he hurt her, if he shamed her. Did *she* care when she shamed him with her insults?

Jenny braced her hands against his chest and shoved at him furiously, but her efforts were insignificant against his superior strength.

He laughed softly in the darkness. "Girl, don't you know that your fighting me is only adding to my pleasure?" he murmured as he felt her soft hips squirm against his hardened body.

"How dare you be so insolent?" she cried.

"And why shouldn't I dare, being the man I am?

Especially after the way you've teased me with your soft beauty and your hot eyes and your damnable virtue. If you were anyone else I would have taken you by now."

His arms were like iron bands imprisoning her. He forced her mouth to open and admit his tongue so that it could mate with hers. Again and again Blade forced Jenny to accept the bold intimacy of his mouth, the wanton caresses of his hands as they slid over her. His fingers unbuttoned her blouse and slid the edges aside so that his hands could knead the soft flesh of her breasts.

Jenny felt as though she would faint with desire as his mouth continued its assault upon her lips and throat with long, flaming kisses, his tongue flicking along the base of her earlobe. He pushed her blouse down over her arms and it fell to the ground. He held her bra beneath her breasts so that it cupped them into rounded globes that sprang enticingly forward, their pink nipples so temptingly succulent he could not long resist lowering his mouth to feast upon them.

"Don't. Oh, Blade, don't!" she cried as his lips came nearer, but when he nuzzled his head gently between her breasts, the pleasure was almost more than Jenny could stand. She moaned, and buried her hands in his rich golden hair as she felt his tongue slide in a rough caress against the tips of her breasts, stroking them, licking them until spasms of longing made her forget all save the raw quivering of her skin beneath his tongue and the warm whisper of his ragged breath as it fell upon her flesh. His fierce wild anger burned through her as passionately and as primitively as did his desire, and everything he did dissolved her pious resolve to fight him.

She shouldn't let him do these things when there was no love between them, when it seemed almost that he hated her. But she scarcely knew who she was or who he was, so lost was she in this new, strange world of swaying rapture. She only knew that she ached for his touch and for his kisses, that she reveled in the savage hunger he had for her.

At last he lifted his mouth from her body. Bereft at the loss of his warmth, she stumbled backward against a huge rock. He was shaking and breathing hard, but he made no move to touch her again. It was as if he knew that if he did, he would not be able to stop himself from taking her.

"Do you know what it does to me to want you and to know you don't think I'm good enough for you? This may surprise you, Jenny Zachery, but loving you would be no good for me either, with you despising yourself and me for what's always been between us." He ran his hands wearily through his golden hair in an agitated motion. "Nothing's changed since you slept with me ten years ago and then married Dean because you thought I was trash."

"But that's not why I married Dean."

"The hell it isn't. You may want me in bed, but out of it you want a man like Dean or Kilpatrick at your side. I'm good enough for a secret affair but not good enough to be seen with. Oh, I know my place, Jenny girl. It's a wound that's raw and burns like hellfire deep inside me. You hate the way you feel about me, and that makes me feel worse than anything anyone else in Zachery Falls could ever say or do."

With that, he turned and left her staring after him feeling more terribly forlorn than she'd ever felt in her life.

Stooping, she reached for her blouse to cover herself.

She was on fire from the wondrous feelings his touch had aroused, yet he actually believed that she scorned his touch, that she thought him beneath her.

Oh, but he was wrong. That wasn't how she felt at all, but would he ever give her the chance to tell him? And would he believe her if she did?

7

Blade returned to the ranch house and stormed up the stairs to his apartment. He arrived home long before Jenny, because after he'd left her she had put herself back together and rejoined the party as if nothing out of the ordinary had happened, as if she weren't upset in the least.

Was she so icy, so untouchable? Her calm was unendurable when his own emotions were in such chaotic fury.

He had asked one of the waiters to drive the tractor back, because after his outburst with Jenny in the woods, Blade knew he was incapable of suffering through the rest of the cookout with the women joking lightly and teasing him, with the music and dancing. But most of all it was Jenny's presence that drove him to seek the sanctuary of his spartan room while he was plunged into his own private hell.

Damnation! How was it that a woman could crawl under a man's skin and cling there for all eternity? There was no losing her, no fighting her. It seemed he'd always been shackled to her. Even when he kissed her in frustration and fury, she could make his blood boil with desire as other women far more beautiful and willing could not. What was it Jenny had? It shook him to the core of his being, this blind, insane wanting. But then, Jenny had always been able to do that to him. Only tonight he hated her for it, and he hated himself as well for the need that consumed him.

He wished he were back in the Marines, a million miles from Zachery Falls and Jenny. But then the memories came flooding back, memories of dirt and flies and the incessant roar of artillery, the stench of oil burning, the feel of a tiny body limp in his arms—all these things came flooding back with shattering force, and as always he deliberately shut the war and all its horror out. He did not wish to be back there at all. He wanted to be home and at peace.

And what he wanted most of all was Jenny beneath him in his bed. He wanted her naked body clinging to his, her silken brown hair rippling across his pillow and entwined in his fingers, the scents of their bodies mingled, the essence of his manhood plunged deep within her. He wanted to hear her whisper love words and moan with passion as she writhed and twisted in his arms. He wanted her to need him as he needed her. He imagined her begging him for the pleasure he could give her, pleading for the ecstasy of his lovemaking, and feeling unashamed about his loving her.

He suppressed the tantalizing vision because it made his blood rise again with desire that would never be satisfied. What a joke it all was, really. Blade laughed bitterly, mocking himself. How everyone in Zachery Falls would laugh if they knew the truth: that tough Blade Taylor, who'd always had a way with women, was pining after a preacher's daughter he couldn't have. It was only what he so richly deserved for all his badness, they would have said, and maybe it was.

Blade pushed open the door and stepped inside. The room smelled of cigarette smoke and a rich, stifling perfume that was all too familiar to him. The tip of a cigarette glowed in the darkness near his bed.

"I thought you'd never come home," Susan purred throatily. "I've been waiting for you, Blade."

"So I see," came his dry reply. "I didn't notice your car."

"It's out back, behind the garage. I didn't want to block the drive. Besides, I wanted to surprise you."

"Well, you certainly did."

"Cigarette?"

"Don't mind if I do."

He went over to the bed, knelt, and struck a match. In the light of the flame their eyes met, and hers were heavy with invitation and desire. The dress she wore was low cut, and had a slit that exposed one thigh. She curved her leg, and his hot gaze slid down the length of it as he stood up again.

Oh, Lord, he thought wearily.

"You haven't called me, Blade. Not in a long time."

Blade had never liked being chased, but then, women like Susan never understood that sort of reticence in a man. "I've been busy," he said mildly.

"Who'd ever have thought Caleb would have left part of the ranch to you in his will? Why didn't you come back to stay after he died, Blade?"

"There wasn't any reason to. Dean was here, taking care of things."

"So you're a rich man. Funny how things work out."

"Life's a joke, all right," Blade agreed in a lazy voice, dragging deeply on his cigarette. "And mine more than most." Only he didn't feel like laughing. Not at the moment, anyway.

"Aren't you even just a little bit glad I came all the way out here to see you tonight, Blade?" she asked ever so silkily, seeking to draw his attention back to herself. "I've been missing you."

She reached out and laid a hand on his sleeve, and he felt the imprint of her soft fingers burn his arm. He stared at the slender hand clutching him, surprised at his lack of response.

His need for Jenny was still a hot, churning force inside him, and Susan's invitation couldn't have been more blatant. Susan was beautiful, ripe and blonde and lush, more beautiful than Jenny, really. He knew too well the pleasure Susan could give him, but he did not want her. His gaze wandered again over her sexily exposed leg.

Susan *was* lovely. But Blade, for all his need of a woman, felt only a deep reluctance toward Susan. Because despite his anger toward Jenny, it was Jenny he loved, Jenny he wanted. And he didn't want Jenny finding Susan here in his room.

"Susan," he began gently. He had no wish to hurt her.

He sat down on the bed beside her to explain again what he'd told her that first afternoon, that they could only be friends. But she misinterpreted his coming to her, and she swayed toward him, her arms encircling his broad shoulders. Before he could say or do anything to stop her, she'd leaned forward and kissed him.

Jenny parked in front of the house and sat in the darkness for a long while, trying to get up the nerve to go over to Blade's room. There would never be an easier time to face him than now, she supposed. She glanced up at his window and saw a faint glimmer of light behind the shade. His Bronco was in the drive.

She had to convince him that he was wrong about her, and explain that she'd been wrong as well. She hadn't known how he'd felt, and because she hadn't known, she'd unwittingly hurt him. She had to make him understand that she didn't think of him the way he thought she did; it was her own feelings that confused her and made her feel guilty, not his bad reputation. She'd never believed in that, anyway.

As she climbed the narrow stairs, her heart beat faster with fear at the thought of facing him. He had been so formidably angry at the cookout. She felt anguished at the thought that he might never forgive her for what she'd done.

His door was ajar, and she peered inside uncertainly, feeling shy and more afraid than ever. The hand she lifted to push the door open further froze in midair. What she saw in the dim light made her blood run cold.

Everything seemed to blacken like burning paper crinkling in a dark fire, and for an instant, she thought she would faint. She couldn't tear her eyes from the sight of Blade and Susan on the bed, kissing. Jenny saw Susan's arms twined around Blade's broad back, and the long curve of her naked leg. They were still dressed, but it took no imagination to know where a kiss between a man like

Blade Taylor and a woman like Susan Harper would inevitably lead.

Somehow Jenny managed to stumble backward in silence. She felt sick with confusion, jealousy, and betrayal. It seemed unbelievable to Jenny that Blade had made love to her so passionately in the woods and then gone to Susan as if his feelings for her meant nothing. Oh, how could he? How could he?

So, everybody was right about him. Any woman would do for him as long as she could be had easily. Only a fool would go and fall in love with a man like him—because all Blade would do was break such a woman's heart.

Was she in love with him? Jenny squashed that idea at once. Of course she wasn't. Love was a noble emotion, not the surging of meaningless passion that she felt for Blade. But the anguish she felt was as real as if she were truly in love.

Tears blinded Jenny as she ran to the house and shut herself inside her own room. How naive she was to have believed in Blade even for a moment, to have believed that there was anything fine and noble in his coming back and helping her with the ranch. What a laugh. The worst was that even after finding Susan in his arms, Jenny still wanted him with that same aching need, and it was even stronger than before.

A sound on the stair made Blade remember himself, and he finally managed to disengage Susan's arms. Pushing her away, he stood up.

"You'd better go, Susan," was all he said.

"Go?" She stared at him incredulously and slid her leg along the bed to bring his attention to it.

"There can't ever be anything between us," he said hoarsely, thinking himself insane for not making love to Susan when he was in such acute need of a woman.

"Blade, you can't mean that."

"But I do. I told you before I only wanted to be friends."

"I know, but—"

"Believe me, Susan, you deserve someone who can love you. And I can't. You ought to try and work things out with Bill."

"I don't want Bill, if I can have you. Is there someone else?" When he said nothing, she spoke slyly. "It's true what they're saying in town, isn't it? That it's Jenny Zachery you want. And maybe you've already had her."

"Don't talk about her," he snapped, admitting nothing, but his fierce anger told Susan she'd hit upon the truth.

"So it *is* Jenny!" Susan jumped up angrily. "You think you're too good for me now, don't you? Because I have a traveling job and kids I see every other weekend. Isn't that a laugh, Blade Taylor thinking he's better than Susan Harper!"

"I think you'd better be going, Susan."

"What can you possibly see in a woman as spineless as Jenny Zachery? She doesn't even know what to do with a man like Mike Kilpatrick, much less a full-blooded male like you. Well, I feel sorry for you, Blade Taylor," Susan finished spitefully, "the way you've always hated all the goody-goody gossips of Zachery Falls, because she's the worst of the lot. I'll bet she despises you and always will."

"I think you've said more than enough," Blade said grimly.

From the bleak look on his handsome face, Susan took

cruel satisfaction in the belief that she had. Then she walked out and banged the door shut behind her.

The rest of the weekend passed dismally for Jenny. She had accepted a date with Mike to go to the town's annual dance. Mike was as nice as always, but being with him and realizing how empty she felt away from Blade only made Jenny feel worse than ever. She noticed for the first time that people were staring at her, newly curious about her because of Blade, but only one person was bold enough to say anything. Cindy Ruthers was a sly, plump girl with an envious, gossipy nature, and she waited until Mike was at the bar with the men, leaving Jenny alone.

"Didn't expect to see you with Mike ever again," Cindy said, her voice furtive and eager as she walked up to Jenny.

Cindy had never been one of Jenny's friends, and Jenny turned on her defensively. "Why not?"

"Well, you know folks are saying that you and Blade—"

"You shouldn't pay attention to gossip," Jenny snapped.

"It's hard for a girl not to listen when the talk's about a man like Blade. But then you'd be one to know what I mean."

"I don't like gossip, and it's not true. Blade's not bad."

"I wasn't saying he was." Beneath the crop of frizzy ringlets that seemed to sprout from her forehead, Cindy's black eyes were bright and avid.

"Then what are you saying, Cindy Ruthers?"

"I was only wondering what it's like, you and he out there all alone when he's always been one for the women."

"Since you know so much, you should realize that Blade has no need to make up to a stick like me when he could have any woman, especially when all the other women in town are so much more interested in him than I am."

"Oh, I wouldn't be so sure of that," Cindy said.

"We're business partners, Blade and I. That's all, and he has as much right to live on the ranch as I do. As for being alone with him, I practically never see him. He works all the time. And Maria lives in the house with me and Cathy, and then there's everyone else at the resort."

Cindy looked at her, and her sharp black eyes were round with disbelief. "Well, Jenny, all it takes is a match to make a stick catch fire, and Blade Taylor's pure dynamite." And with that she walked away, leaving Jenny alone once more.

Jenny went to church on Sunday morning. After the service she ate lunch with Mike and his friends at the Bluebonnet Café. That afternoon she drove into San Antonio and took Cathy to the zoo. All weekend she tried not to think of Blade, but the memory of seeing him with Susan was a constant torment.

Jenny saw little of Blade during the week that followed, although she was deeply aware of him when she did. He seemed as determined to avoid her as she was to avoid him. For that at least she should have been thankful, but of course she wasn't. She kept wondering where he was and who he was with, and despite her determination to hate him, she longed to see him.

The next Saturday afternoon, before she was to get ready for yet another date with Mike, she saw a double horsetrailer parked near the barn. When she went to investigate, she found Blade slowly leading a black thoroughbred stallion with the look of the devil in his eyes down the length of the corral.

"Blade, what are you doing?" she asked in surprise as she stepped inside the corral and watched him struggle with the horse, talking soothingly all the while. She watched with fascination the ripple of muscles along Blade's broad back, as well.

They were magnificent, the horse and the man, two splendid male specimens, each as wild and determined to have his way as the other. Each was a challenge to the other.

"Keep clear of Mac, Jenny. He's half wild from not having been ridden in over a year. I bought him and a mare at that cattle sale I went to two weeks ago. They've just been delivered. You'll enjoy the mare—Red, they called her—but I'll have to tame Mac—if that's even possible—before I can ride him."

"Mac. That's a strange name for a horse."

"He's a strange horse, and not noted for the most pleasant of dispositions."

"But Mac?"

"It stands for Machiavelli. You may remember that a few hundred years ago there was a certain unscrupulously cunning and rather deceptive Italian statesman—"

"Oh, dear."

"Mac has more in common with that individual than his name, I'm afraid."

He ignored Jenny after that and concentrated on the horse, talking gently, stroking the sleek black neck. Blade knew horses as well as he knew women, and if Mac could be gentled, he was the man who could do it. As she watched him work with the horse, Jenny forgot for a moment her fierce rage and her feelings of humiliation over his involvement with Susan, and longed for him to speak as softly and to touch her as gently as he caressed the horse. But he continued to ignore her, until finally she remembered that she wanted to set her hair before her date with Mike.

As she was leaving the corral she accidentally brushed against three long boards that were leaning against the fence. The lumber had been stacked there carelessly by Chuck, who had been planning to use the boards to patch a hole in the barn wall. The heavy boards crashed to the ground in a thunderous clatter, and Jenny jumped aside so they would not strike her.

From behind her she heard Mac's wild scream as he broke loose from Blade.

"Jenny, watch out!" Blade cried hoarsely.

She whirled in time to see Blade lunge in front of the horse to save her from being trampled. Hooves thudded heavily against flesh and earth and because of Blade's quick action the horse swerved, narrowly missing Jenny before he sprang forward and galloped past her out of the gate that she had opened.

Jenny gave no thought to the horse, but rushed over to where Blade lay on the ground. He sat up slowly, his mouth a thin, tight line that told her he was in pain. A trickle of blood ran the length of his cheek.

She knelt beside him in the dirt, touching his bruised and bloodied cheek with her fingertips.

"Blade, are you all right?" She was white and ill at the thought of how close he'd come to being ground into bloody pulp by the savage hooves. "Oh, Blade—"

" 'All right,' is not exactly the way I'd describe how I'm feeling at the moment," he said a bit ruefully, rubbing his cheek. But he looked at her, and his blue eyes were as startlingly vivid as ever as he attempted one of his jaunty smiles.

His hand closed over hers tightly, and his expression was both fierce and gentle at the same time.

"That was close," he said, his grip tightening on her hand as if to assure himself of her safety. "Too damn close." She felt his hand shaking in hers, but she didn't know of the fear that tore at him inside when he thought of her being injured. "Stay away from the barn for now, until that demon is tamed," he said in abrupt dismissal.

He rose and helped her up as well. Then he moved past her, his strides long and easy, despite his aches and pains. She didn't know that he was leaving because his feelings for her were so intense that they were barely under control.

"Blade—"

He turned, and the sunshine was brilliant in his golden hair. She noted the bruise on his cheek and the dark stain on his shirt where the horse had knocked him to the ground. He could have been killed because of her. Blade killed! At the thought a feeling as dark as death itself wrenched her heart, and she realized how utterly lost she would feel if anything happened to him.

"You're not going after the stallion," she said desperately.

"I damn sure am."

"Please, Blade, you might get hurt."

The sympathy in her voice upset him, because any passion from her reminded him of the feelings she had for him that she did not want to have. His own emotions were raw and too near the surface, and he could not keep the anger out of his low tone.

"And why would you care about that, Jenny? Why

aren't you inside getting ready for your date with Kilpat-rick? I thought he was the type to arouse your womanly concern while I only arouse feelings you're ashamed of."

"How did you know about my date with Mike?" she asked weakly. His rough tone hurt her.

"Word travels fast around here. Or did you forget that there are no secrets in Zachery Falls? Maybe I should date someone myself, so people won't link us together. Why I haven't gotten involved with another woman since I came to live out here is beyond me."

"But you are!" she wanted to cry out, thinking of Susan. So he was a liar as well as a womanizer; doubtless he was several other equally detestable things as well.

"I guess it's the wisest thing," Blade continued, "your going out with Kilpatrick. Maybe it'll hush the talk about us, and you'll be able to hold up your head in town again." He smiled derisively. "Maybe, just maybe, you'll wash away the taint of your association with me."

Jenny was remembering how she'd felt when she'd seen him kissing Susan, and suddenly she was filled anew with hurt and resentment toward him. How could he chase women so casually? It was infuriating and humiliat-ing to care so much for a man who cared nothing for her. Suddenly the need to hurt him as he had hurt her overwhelmed her.

"Yes," she agreed passionately. "I hope it will wash away the taint of you, Blade Taylor. Any woman would be proud to be seen with a man like Mike. He's a gentleman. He respects me. Whereas you . . . all you know how to do is drag a woman down to your own level until she has no self-respect or pride left."

Blade stood very still, and he looked at her for a long time as the breeze ruffled his golden hair. There was a taut intensity about him that unnerved her and made her feel ashamed of what she'd said. It did no good to think that he had driven her to say it because he'd made love to her that night and then been with Susan such a short time later. Suddenly Jenny felt afraid as Blade stalked toward her. The stillness was gone from his face and in its place was an angry violence.

Jenny stumbled as she tried to back away from him, but Blade caught her, yanking her against him.

"Wash this away if you can," he muttered as he brought his mouth down hard upon hers and forced the curves of her body to melt against his male contours. She felt the hard muscles of his thighs against her body, the power of his chest crushing her breasts. His lips were hot and familiar, his embrace deliberately insolent, but everything he did stirred a warm tide of delirious feeling that both bewildered and frightened her. She went limp, unresisting, as thrilling quivers coursed through her, and she forgot everything but Blade and his hands and mouth moving over her.

As always his lovemaking brought a familiar blaze of hunger to them both, even though she knew he was using her, demeaning her. He kissed her with slow, hot lips, and she shivered despite the warmth of the day. He arched her body against his own, and his mouth traveled down her throat to the hollow between her breasts. His lips were like raw flames flicking her insides until she was molten with arousal. She moaned in surrender, and more than anything she longed for him to lift her into his arms and carry her to some private place and make love to her. She thought of the hayloft in the barn, plump and soft with fresh hay. But he didn't do that.

Very slowly he released her and pushed her away, but passion was throbbing in them both. His desire made him even angrier at himself and at her, while hers deepened her feelings of humiliation, because she believed she meant no more to him than Susan Harper did, and maybe not as much.

"I hate you," she said in a low voice choked with pain. "I won't be treated like one of your cheap women!"

"Won't you? You asked for that, you know. What in the hell did you think you were doing?" he demanded. "Coming out here, watching me all afternoon? Why the hell don't you stay away from me if you despise me? If you don't want my kisses? If you don't want me? I damn sure try to keep clear of you. Why don't you chase after Kilpatrick if he's the man you really want?"

Hurt, she was defiant. "That's exactly what I intend to do."

"And do *his* kisses make you feel like fainting? I could have taken you now, and you know it. As easily as I've ever taken any woman. More easily than some."

It galled her to hear the truth about herself put in such blunt terms, and she hated him for it. "There's no reason to compare yourself to Mike. You and he aren't in the same league at all. Mike's a gentleman," she replied huffily as if that said everything.

Blade's lips curled. "So you've said, but I'm surprised that a girl of your unbridled, passionate nature doesn't find that a bit of a bore."

"How did you kn—" She caught herself in the nick of time. "You don't know me at all. Not really."

"Don't I?" His gaze was hot and impertinent, his smile knowing, and she realized that he was remembering that long ago afternoon he'd made love to her, when he'd explored every part of her with his mouth and tongue. "And I thought I knew you as well as any man," he said with a smile. Then he shrugged. "But nice as it is discussing some of my most cherished memories of you,

I guess I'd better go after Mac before he gallops over the county line."

He was leaving. Dismissing her as though she were of no consequence. The desire to have the last word swelled within her breast.

"Blade Taylor, if you're stubborn enough to go after that horse, I hope he tramples you into the ground and makes raw meat of you," she cried, still furious.

He merely smiled sardonically. "How nice. And to think all these visions of homicide and gore come from the sweet, pure lips of a preacher's daughter."

"I hope you break your fool neck! I hope it snaps like a twig!"

He laughed curtly.

"I do!"

"Oh, I believe you, but you can save your insults, Jenny." His voice was silky. "You know, a man can only die once."

"Well, that's certainly a pity in your case."

"So I've been told," came his dry reply.

He grinned as she stormed past him toward the house. "Cheer up," he called. "This may be your lucky day. I may indeed be trampled into the dust by that four-legged beast. You can come to my funeral. That should really be a jolly event for you and everybody else in Zachery Falls. A pity I won't be there to enjoy making all of you so happy." She heard his laughter following her and quickened her pace.

All too soon she regretted her anger and her insults, but it was too late to apologize. He'd left immediately to search for Mac. As the hours dragged by and he did not return, she began to fret. Maybe a stray hoof had bashed him in the head and he was lying unconscious in a pasture somewhere. The thought made her tense and fearful, but when she considered going to look for him, she reminded herself of how ridiculous it was of her to care, and how humiliated she would feel if he wasn't hurt and he discovered her concern for him.

Oh, he was abominable, and she wished that he'd never come back. Her awareness of him was consuming her. She didn't know how to think anymore. She couldn't even act naturally. It was not her habit to be quarrelsome with anyone; why then did she quarrel with Blade?

Hours later, when Mike was driving her to the party, she saw Blade in the distance, a lonely, broad-shouldered figure silhouetted against a blood red horizon. He was leading the powerful Mac homeward. Deep relief washed through her at the knowledge that he was all right. It wasn't really so much that she cared about Blade that made her glad to see him safe, she told herself quickly. It was just that she would have felt guilty if she'd driven him to serious injury because she'd made him mad.

Jenny did not see Blade again for the rest of the weekend, and she knew that it was deliberate on his part. But she thought of him, and she wondered whose lips he kissed in the sultry darkness, whose body he pressed beneath his against some soft mattress. And when she thought about it, she felt like dying.

On Monday morning Jenny's stomach twisted with dread at the prospect of going to work and seeing Blade on a casual basis throughout the day. So she did the cowardly thing; she called in and said she was sick.

At ten o'clock Jenny was outside playing with Cathy and Heidi in the backyard when she saw Blade's Bronco on the road, heading for the house. A sudden vision of him wrapped in Susan's arms momentarily engulfed her in pain. Then she forced herself to pick up the stuffed bear that Cathy had deliberately dropped in her favorite game of ut-oh. Absently Jenny handed the bear to the little girl, but her attention was riveted to the sound of the truck in the drive.

Blade strode around the corner of the house. His handsome face was dark with concern, but then his look of worry died, and he smiled at the sight of her playing with the golden-haired child. The anger he'd displayed on Saturday afternoon seemed to have vanished. Doubtless, Jenny tortured herself grimly, he'd lost it in the pleasure he'd found in another woman's arms.

Cathy ran from her mother and tumbled into Blade's strong brown arms, and Jenny almost envied her own daughter for the easiness she shared with her uncle. Blade laughed at the child and dropped her bear onto the ground for her. "Ut-oh," he said gently, and Cathy beamed at him before she stooped to retrieve the toy.

Over Cathy's curls, Blade spoke in a low voice to Jenny. "I thought you were sick."

Had he really been so concerned that he'd driven all the way back to the house to see about her? Jenny pushed that sudden, hopeful thought aside. Why was she always determined to see everything he did in such an eternally romantic light? Would she always be such a fool where one man with a rowdy fall of gold hair and a devilish grin and a terrible reputation was concerned?

"I didn't feel like working," she replied stiffly. "But since when is what I do any of your business?"

The light in his eyes died, and she hated the way he looked at her.

"I don't suppose it is," he said slowly. "I'm disappointed in you, though. Not that I haven't always known you were less than perfect. There's your temper, of course, and then there's—" His hot blue gaze slid over her with the look of a man who knew a wanton when he saw one, despite her false pretenses, and Jenny flushed with shame. "Well, suffice it to say that I'm well aware of many of your weaknesses, but this is a new one on me. I never realized you were a quitter."

Jenny compressed her lips in fury. She longed to upbraid him for his insolent glance and insinuations, but how could she, without seeming to be one to protest too much? "The hit dog hollers," her father had always said. "I'm *not* a quitter," she grumbled at last.

He stared at her in frank disbelief. "I don't blame you, though, for quitting. Not really. The resort is in a real mess. Sometimes I feel like giving up myself." He dropped the bear again and Cathy cooed with delight as she toddled after it.

"I'm not giving up!" she cried. "Can't you understand?"

"Oh, so you've decided to take my advice and that of everyone else in Zachery Falls and stay home and persuade this little minx to give up her thumb." He ruffled Cathy's curls and then lifted her high in his arms, teddy bear and all. "I see she's got it in her mouth as usual."

"Thumb, Uncle Blade!" Cathy squealed proudly.

"The hell you say!" Jenny exclaimed. "She's barely two, and she'll stop by herself when she has a mind to. I'm going to work right now."

"I thought you would, when I said that." He was laughing softly, and his laughter made her more furious than anything.

As Jenny drove into work she knew that she had been

tricked. He'd come out to the house and when he'd found her well, he'd goaded her into returning to work despite the fact that it was the last thing she wanted to do. He was insufferable.

Still, deep in that most secret place in her heart, Jenny was glad that he'd cared enough to come after her.

8

⚙⚙⚙⚙⚙⚙⚙⚙⚙

Mr. Taylor would like to see you in his office, Mrs. Zachery," Lilly said with a knowing smile that infuriated Jenny.

"All right," Jenny snapped. This was the fifteenth time she'd been summoned to Blade's office today, or that he'd come to hers on some bit of nonsense. She'd scarcely been able to get a thing done because of all the interruptions.

As she got up from her desk, Jenny was aware of Lilly watching her with a faintly disrespectful look of speculation. It was a look that everyone in Zachery Falls had these days when they glanced at her, even Mike.

Ever since that Monday morning when Blade had come to the ranch house and goaded her into returning to work, his attitude toward her had been blatantly different. Instead of avoiding her, he had begun to deliberately seek her out.

When he inspected the town houses, he insisted that she accompany him. After all, wasn't she his partner? Sometimes they would be alone together inside a town house for more than an hour while he made notes about one thing or another. All that time she would be thinking of the gossip that their being alone together would surely cause, because the maids would watch them go inside and wait to see when they came back out, as well.

Jenny wanted to say something to Blade, but somehow it was too embarrassing a subject to broach with him, especially when he did seem to be working so conscientiously to improve the resort. She could scarcely fault him for his enthusiasm for work that was benefiting so many people—including herself. Not when his efforts were beginning to pay off so handsomely. The monthly gross was steadily and rapidly rising. The resort itself hummed like a well-managed factory, and Blade was the cause of that hum. The staff was happier than they had ever been, and the resort guests constantly praised everything.

But why did he demand that she be with him constantly? Whenever Blade drove into Austin or San Antonio on resort business he invited her to accompany him, saying that he hated to make important decisions without her advice. When she tried to refuse such invitations, he would press her unmercifully until she accepted. Of course that was never too difficult for him, because she wanted to go with him despite the fact that it made people question their relationship.

The telephone line between their offices buzzed continually when they were both at the resort. It seemed that Blade could no longer make the most inconsequential decision without first seeking her opinion. What irritated her the most was the fact that his attention and friendliness thrilled her, when she knew it all meant nothing to him.

In the evenings he came up to the ranch house on the pretense of working with her on various resort projects, but in reality he did little work. He talked to her and he played with Cathy, and all the while Jenny was aware of Maria watching them with a knowing smile on her face, the same smile that everyone in Zachery Falls wore these days when they saw her with Blade.

Blade took her horseback riding as well, to inspect the ranch, he said. But just what he was inspecting she was never sure. Mac was still half wild, and it frightened her when Blade insisted upon riding him.

They rode everywhere together, and were sometimes gone for hours on Saturday or Sunday afternoons. Occasionally they rode to the cemetery. Once he took her to the cabin that he and Caleb and Dean had used whenever they'd gone hunting on the most remote and wildest section of the ranch. To her surprise, it was clean and neatly furnished, and Blade admitted that he'd used it more than once since he'd come back when he'd felt the need to get off by himself. To her amazement, she learned that that was where he'd spent his first few nights in town before he'd moved into the apartment over the garage. Jenny could not help remembering all the times she'd believed he was with a woman. Had he really been at the cabin seeking solitude?

Blade had not touched Jenny physically since that afternoon in the corral, but every time he looked at her there was a hot light in his eyes that he no longer made any effort to conceal from her or anyone else. He watched her constantly. He seemed to be waiting for something, but she didn't know what. She only knew that she felt nervous herself, and that this change in him made her feel strangely expectant.

Once when they were in town together, Susan drove by in her red Porsche, but when she saw Blade with Jenny, she looked the other way and didn't return his wave.

Jenny wondered about that. She even asked Blade about it.

"Aren't you speaking to Susan these days?"

"I'm speaking. Apparently she's not," he returned indifferently, as though the subject of Susan held not the slightest interest for him.

"I hear she's dating her ex-husband again."

"I hope they get back together, for their children's sake, and for Susan's too," Blade said easily, without a trace of jealousy. "You know, she only sees her kids every other weekend. Children need more mothering than that."

"But I thought you two—"

Blue eyes slanted toward Jenny. "You thought wrong."

"Everybody said—"

"Everybody in this town would do a hell of a lot better if they would start minding their own business instead of mine."

Something in Blade's voice told Jenny that the subject of Susan Harper was closed. Jenny wished she could forget the way he'd passionately kissed Susan that night on his bed as easily as he apparently could, but the memory of that naked leg and their wanton embrace stayed in her mind, haunting her, bringing her endless pain. It prevented her from believing that Blade could ever really love one woman. Had he not passionately proclaimed his need for Jenny and then taken Susan into his arms the very same night? And now he had abandoned Susan as well. It was apparent that, for all his charismatic appeal and overwhelming maleness, he lacked the ability to love and be true to one woman. But she'd always known that, and Jenny reminded herself that she didn't love Blade, however appealing she found him physically. Why should his inability to be faithful trouble her so, when her own feelings for him were equally shallow?

In short, she was more confused than ever about Blade as she walked briskly down the hall to his office to answer this latest interruption of her day. Her cheeks were crimson in irritation, and Chuck grinned knowingly as she passed him, misinterpreting completely the reason for her color. Chuck's smile only made her more angry at Blade because it was his fault that people now thought the worst of her.

As she strode into Blade's office she was determined to tell him that she couldn't get a thing done when he constantly interrupted her. Her hot words died in her throat the minute she saw that he was not alone. His office was crowded with law officers, and the atmosphere was tense.

Blade, who'd been sitting behind his desk with an air of lazy unconcern, stood up, and came toward her to escort her inside. Everyone in the room was as conscious as she of the brown hand resting possessively at the back of her waist and the warm white smile that was meant only for her.

"Gentlemen, sheriff," Blade said easily, his hand still upon Jenny's waist. "I'm sure you all know my partner,

Jenny." Blade's blue gaze was deliberately bold and intimate as he glanced toward her again.

Blade never called her Mrs. Zachery any more in front of people, as he had for so long, and there was no mistake in anyone's mind that Blade Taylor was seriously interested in her as a woman.

Everyone nodded and smiled at Jenny—that is, everyone except a frail-looking boy of about eighteen who was handcuffed and seated beside Sheriff Blunzer. He sat slumped in his chair with his black eyes downcast, but occasionally he looked up, tossing his head so that his long black hair didn't tumble over his eyes, as he glared around the room with hatred.

"Blade, what's going on? Why is that boy—"

"We've solved the mystery of the stolen television sets," Blade explained succinctly. "I've spent several weekends and nights inside vacant town houses, trying to catch the thief, and last night it paid off. I caught Rick here letting himself into Town House 48 and unhooking the cable of a television set. He finally admitted to me that he stole a set of town house keys from one of the maids he's been dating, and he's been stealing television sets one by one on Sunday afternoons, whenever he and his family needed the money."

The boy stared angrily at Blade and then at Jenny as if he resented being talked about.

"We have enough hard evidence to put him in prison for years, ma'am," Sheriff Blunzer said importantly, "if only you'll agree to press charges."

"Of course I'll agree, if that's what Mr. Taylor wants to do."

Jenny stared at the boy. It was horrible to think of one so young having to go to prison.

"That's just the problem," Blunzer said. "That's not what Mr. Taylor wants to do. I can't get him to press charges."

"What?" Jenny looked up at Blade in surprise.

"Jenny," Blade began, "I've talked to the boy, and to his mother. Their situation really is quite desperate. There are five children in the family. The father drinks. This boy, Rick, has been the sole support of the family for two years, ever since he dropped out of school to go to work. Four months ago he lost his job, and he hasn't been able to get another one. His mother's been sick."

"But surely there are agencies that can help . . . money . . ."

"It wasn't enough. I want to pay the town house owners myself for the television sets, and personally take custody of the boy. I'll hire him and take a small amount out of his salary each week against the price of the stolen sets."

Jenny stared at the angry, defiant boy, filled with doubt at the wisdom of Blade's assuming responsibility for him. What if he hurt someone? A hotel guest? Cathy? At the very least, he'd probably steal from them again.

"Blade, are you sure this is what you want to do?"

Blade glanced at the boy, and his blue eyes were filled with a look of profound compassion and empathy. "I'm very sure," he said at last.

Sheriff Blunzer snorted. "You'll be sorry, Mr. Taylor. You don't know what you're doing. His dad's a drunk. His mother's a liar. This boy's a thief. He'll likely turn out to be as trashy as his folks."

The boy tried to lunge out of his chair like a wild animal, but two deputies restrained him.

Blade stared thoughtfully at the sheriff and at the

fierce, proud anger of the boy for a long moment. "You called him trash. In case you don't remember, sheriff, that's what everyone has always labeled me."

An hour later, Blade, Jenny, and Rick were alone in Blade's office. Rick was rubbing wrists that were finally free of manacles and staring at the floor.

"Why'd you do it, Taylor?" Rick muttered in a voice that was scarcely audible.

"Maybe I want to give you a chance to prove you're not what Blunzer says."

"I don't want your charity."

"It's not exactly charity," Blade said mildly. "You might say that I'm repaying an old debt."

"You don't owe me nothin', 'cause I never did nothin' for nobody, especially not for you."

"It's not the kind of debt you repay to the person you owe. Besides, the man I owe is dead."

"I could run, Taylor, you know that. Or steal you blind, if I had a mind to," Rick said angrily.

"You'd be cutting your own throat and that of your family, and I'd see that you're caught, Rick, because you're my responsibility now. And I take my responsibilities seriously. I don't like people stealing from me. Not you. Not anybody. If you're smart, you won't even think about stealing again. You'll work and prove to me and everybody else around here that you're made of something better than they think you are. Or maybe you *are* what Blunzer thinks."

"I'm not!"

"That won't be easy to prove. From what I hear, people around here are pretty set against you."

"I'll prove it."

"What kind of job would you like?" Blade asked, changing the subject. "You'll start at the bottom, of course, but we've got all sorts of jobs around here."

There was a long pause. At last Rick spoke, and there was less anger in his voice than before. "I've always had a way with horses, Mr. Taylor."

Blade smiled. "Have you now? Then that's settled. Report to the stables in the morning. Eight o'clock sharp. For now, go home and tell your mother about our agreement."

"You mean I'm free to go?"

Rick looked up and Blade smiled.

"There's one thing you need to learn about me, Johnson. I don't like repeating myself. Now get out of here."

Rick scrambled out of the room.

Jenny turned to Blade and their eyes met. It was strange, how incredibly wonderful she felt.

"Blade, that was very kind of you, trying to do something for that boy."

He merely shrugged. Then he grinned at her, and there was a hint of mischief in his eyes. "It was nothing, really. Chalk it up as my good deed for the day. And put it on the same mental blackboard where you're always listing my bad deeds, okay?"

"None of the more virtuous citizens of Zachery Falls would have put themselves to such an expense for a stranger, or considered taking such a risk," she said.

"Then maybe they aren't so virtuous as they think they are. It would never occur to them that there's good in someone even after he's made a mistake or two—like Rick Johnson. Not that I care what they think anymore."

She reached out and took Blade's hand. With anyone

else it might have been no more than a meaningless, friendly gesture, but as always between them there was the spark of something else in their lightest touch. His arms came around her in sudden passion. His expression was intense; his lips hovered inches above hers, and Jenny felt oddly breathless as he lowered his mouth, capturing hers in a kiss that was hungry with frustration because he had not kissed her or held her in weeks.

He realized at once that it was unwise to kiss her. It was contrary to his plan, but the expression on her face had been too soft and beautiful to resist. It was heaven to feel her soft lips under his without any anger or shame between them. Her arms encircled his waist, and she pressed herself against him as if her need was as blind and overwhelming as his, as if this time she couldn't deny the rising tide of desire in herself.

Blade deepened the kiss. His tongue curled inside her mouth, touching the tip of hers. His loins felt as hot as melting wax as she eagerly returned his kisses. It satisfied something deep within him to know that she wanted him as desperately as he wanted her, despite all her protests.

She offered herself to him without restraint. Tiny moans of pleasure and excitement escaped her lips. All her innate sensuality was aroused, and the feel of her slim body against his own, the body that had haunted his dreams, drove him insane with a fierce desire to possess her. Her body was his for the moment; the taut breasts, the long legs, the sweet hips.

Neither spoke; their responses were wordless and instinctive. Though there were no avowals of love because each was too proud to betray himself aloud, the intensity of their feelings was revealed in every caress, in every kiss.

Blade longed to be alone with her, in some remote,

private place. God, it had been so long since he'd had a woman. His loins were on fire.

Suddenly Blade's secretary burst through the door, and the intimate moment was shattered.

"Oh, I'm sorry," Nancy exclaimed, in blushing confusion. "I thought you were alone, Mr. Taylor."

Blade's arms dropped slowly away, and Jenny flushed in mortification to have been discovered kissing him. She felt weak, dazed. How could Blade look so calm? He looked as if he didn't mind the interruption in the least, while she felt ravaged. She didn't notice that his hands were knotted into hard fists against his thighs.

"What is it, Nancy?" he asked smoothly.

"There's a Mr. Thomas to see you, Mr. Taylor, about the possibility of using Woodlands Hideaway as a conference site for his computer seminar."

"Oh, yes. I'm afraid that appointment completely slipped my mind."

Nancy flushed prettily as she darted a glance at Jenny, who was frantically pinning her hair back into its normally tidy bun.

"Show him in, after Jenny leaves. She and I have not quite finished our . . . er . . . our business discussion," Blade said with a bold smile.

The door clicked softly as Nancy exited.

Jenny whirled on him. "How could you?"

He grinned. "How could I what?"

"Act like nothing was wrong!"

"Nothing is."

His casual attitude infuriated her even more. "Nothing except that my reputation is in shreds."

"It already was, or hadn't you noticed?"

"You mean you knew all along that your behavior was making people believe that you and I are lovers?"

"This should finally prove how little a person has to do in this town to be labeled 'bad.' "

"But I've done nothing wrong."

His smile was devilish. "Exactly."

"You're a rogue."

"I've been told that before."

"And you don't care?"

"Maybe I learned a long time ago, Jenny, that I can't help what people say about me."

"You've never even tried to change."

"Maybe I'm satisfied with the person I am. Why should I change just because a lot of meddling busybodies think I should?"

"My reputation is in shreds because of you, and you stand there grinning, acting like you've done something to be proud of. You don't care what you've done to me."

"No, as a matter of fact, I don't. I've lived with a bad reputation for years. Now that you've lost yours, there's less to keep us apart. The bridge between your virtue and my sin is gone, and you're on my side of the river now, girl. Who knows, maybe you'll learn to enjoy the freedom you'll gain from the loss of that reputation you think so precious. For one thing, now you can share my bed without worrying what everyone thinks. They already think the worst."

"You planned this!"

"Hell, Jenny, you were never the girl they thought in the first place, were you? So staid and everlastingly proper, so faithful to my brother, Dean?" Her cheeks flamed at the knowledge in his eyes. "Why don't you try being yourself for a change? You may find that's a better way to live than worrying about what other people think all the time."

"I hate you, Blade Taylor. You've deliberately ruined my life."

"Oh, I wasn't trying to ruin it."

"Well, you have."

"Are you so sure? Tell me that again tonight, after we—"

She was too angry to allow him to finish. "For your information, I'm through with you for good. I have no intention of letting you touch me again, tonight or any other night."

"Then I'll have to change your mind about that, won't I?"

"You—" She choked back her words, realizing there was absolutely nothing she could say to take him down a notch.

He merely smiled as she stormed out the door, but there was a wealth of promise in his bold blue eyes.

That evening Mike dropped by the ranch house unexpectedly. When Jenny opened the front door, the sinking sun was golden on the hills. Maria had taken Cathy to the stables to watch Blade while he was exercising Mac.

"Why, Mike, it's so nice to see you," Jenny said, coming out onto the porch. "Can you stay for a while? Would you like a cool drink? We could sit out on the swing and talk. You know we haven't done that in ages." In the back of her mind was the cowardly notion of using Mike as a shield to hide behind when Blade made his inevitable return to the house.

"This isn't exactly a social call."

She hadn't thought it was.

"I want to talk to you, Jenny, about the rumors concerning you and Blade Taylor."

Jenny stiffened as she led him to the swing. "I don't

care to discuss that subject with you or anyone else. I haven't done anything wrong, and I'm not in the mood to defend myself."

"I never thought for a minute that you had. But it's an outrage the way Taylor's dragging your reputation through the gutter just by constantly hanging around you and looking at you the way he always looks at his women. He knows what everyone thinks of him around here, and if he were a gentleman, he'd stay clear of you. It's bad enough him coming back and taking what should have been yours and Cathy's, not to mention him freeing criminals so they can run loose."

"What's an outrage is the way people talk about others even when they have no cause," Jenny said heatedly, sidestepping the subject of Blade. It was curious the way it irritated her to hear Mike speak ill of Blade, even when she herself was furious with him.

"I've decided there's only one solution to this problem that will shut people up once and for all," Mike said.

"And what's that?" Jenny asked, perplexed by his softening tone and the warm light in his eyes.

"It's time you got married."

From the darkness behind them came Blade's deep voice as he rode up on Mac.

"My feelings exactly, Kilpatrick. Marry me, Jenny. I'm more than willing to make an honest woman of you."

"I didn't mean that she should marry you, you fool! I meant me," Mike shouted, bolting out of the swing toward Blade.

Mac reared at the sudden movement, and Blade spoke soothingly. "Easy there, boy. Don't go getting skittish on me." To Mike he said, "Kilpatrick, I'll thank you to take your seat again and not go spooking Mac. And as for you marrying Jenny—it's my name hers is linked with, not yours. What would people say, anyhow, about you marrying one of Blade Taylor's women?"

Mike looked as green around the gills as a gasping fish as he sank back onto the swing. Jenny was every bit as angry as Mike was at Blade. How could he make a joke of asking her to marry him and insult her so odiously at the same time? It was obvious he didn't really care about her or he wouldn't speak that way. She clenched her teeth and glared at Blade, hating him most of all for the rippling excitement his teasing remark about matrimony stirred deep within her.

"I wouldn't marry you if you were the last man on earth, Blade Taylor. The very last man!"

"Of course she wouldn't. No virtuous, self-respecting woman would want you, Taylor. Not in this town," Mike interjected smugly, sure of himself on that subject.

Blade laughed down at them both. "This one does," he said pointedly, looking at Jenny. "Tell him, girl. Tell him it's me you want and not him. That it's always been me, even if it's not marriage you want. Tell him that you're my woman."

"You're a liar, Blade Taylor," she cried.

"I'm a lot of things, and not all of them good. But a liar I'm not, as you well know. Tell him, girl, what's between you and me, what's been between us these past ten years, even before you married Dean. Or are you such a tease that you want him eating his heart out over you for the rest of his life?"

Mike turned to Jenny in confusion. "What's he talking about? There's nothing between you two. You always loved Dean."

Jenny clasped her hands over her mouth and gave a

strangled gasp. All she had to do was deny what Blade said. Mike would never take Blade's word against hers. "Mike—" she began, but suddenly she was too choked to speak.

"Tell me Taylor's lying," Mike demanded. His eyes pierced hers.

Something broke inside her, and she just didn't care anymore what people thought of her. She couldn't lie to Mike. She was through trying to live up to the false image of perfection everyone had of her.

"Mike, I—I can't," she admitted at last, "because . . . it's true."

"What?"

"You heard her, Kilpatrick. Now if you don't mind, I'd like a word alone with my . . . er . . . fiancée."

Mike looked venomously at Blade and then stomped down the steps and rushed toward his Cadillac. Jenny hesitated and then ran after him, determined to explain, but when she reached the drive it was choked with dust and exhaust and lit with the red twinkle of disappearing taillights.

"Mike—" She called after him, but he didn't hear. And had he heard, he would not have stopped.

She whirled to run back to the safety of the house, where she could nurse her bruised pride and angry hurt, but she found Blade, magnificently astride the prancing Mac, directly in her path.

Never had Blade seemed more terrifyingly handsome than he did now in the purple twilight. His hair was a shower of gold falling rakishly across his tanned forehead. The first three buttons of his shirt were unfastened, revealing his bronzed chest; his jeans snugly molded his powerful thighs. But it was the look in his eyes that alarmed her. They were dark and yet startlingly vivid, blatantly communicating his sexual desire. Never had he seemed more ruthless or more masculine, and suddenly she was frightened. Nevertheless, she squared her shoulders and said bravely, "Get out of my way and let me pass, Blade Taylor."

He merely laughed, and it was a vibrant, sexy sound. "So you can go inside and sulk? Not on your life."

Jenny hesitated. She was uncomfortably aware of the growing darkness, and of the fact that Maria and Cathy had not yet returned to the house.

"Where's Cathy?" she demanded, sensing the presence of some unnamed, primeval danger.

"There's a children's movie at the lodge, and I sent her to the resort with Maria—so you and I could be alone." His voice was low and husky, and something in its timbre made her feel hot and quivery inside.

Alone. The word repeated itself in her mind, sending out signals of raw, searing danger.

"Without my permission?" she gasped weakly, stalling in a vain effort to divert him.

Blade grinned at that, real amusement dancing in his bold blue eyes. "That's right, Jenny. You and I have a lot to discuss, and I don't want to be distracted by your little angel."

"I'm through talking to you, Blade Taylor!" she cried.

He chuckled. "That, my darling, may be the best idea you've had tonight."

Blade leaned forward and made a clicking sound with his teeth against Mac's flattened ear, and Jenny saw his heels press lightly into his mount as he reined the horse toward her. As his eyes slid over her body, she knew what he wanted, what he intended. There had always been a barely leashed wildness about him, and tonight he wore the look of a man who would take what he wanted with no thought of the consequences.

Without thinking, she began to run from him.

In her jeans and sneakers she was more agile than usual, and she ran with the fleet swiftness of a terrified deer, racing away from the house toward a thick stand of oak and juniper. If only Blade hadn't been between her and the house, she could have gotten inside and locked him out. But what good would that have done? she thought desperately. He knew she was alone. He could easily get inside and overpower her.

Branches tore her hair loose from its bun and it streamed down her back. Still, she ran deeper and deeper into the woods until it was so dark she could scarcely see. She stumbled and fell and picked herself up again. The last rays of the sun were like glimmering ribbons of fire as they filtered among the trees. Behind her she could hear the clatter of Mac's hooves on the loose rocks, and the echo of Blade's hushed laughter.

He was enjoying himself, the devil!

She was right, but she didn't know how much her slim, fleeing form tantalized Blade as she ran before him, how he deliberately held the horse back so that he could watch her slender body dart to and fro between the trees, her long, dark mane swinging wildly about her shoulders. She was as beautiful to him as a wood nymph, with her narrow back, her curving hips, and her long, graceful legs. Every so often a shaft of fire illuminated the exquisite loveliness of her. She was as rare and precious as a blazing jewel, and he was determined to possess her.

At last Blade, longing for the feel of her body crushed to his, grew tired of the game and dug his heels into Mac so that the horse spurted into a mad gallop through the trees after her. Catching up to her, he leaned over and captured her, one arm tightly wrapped around her waist, bringing her up beside him. The warmth of her against him set Blade on fire.

Jenny writhed in his arms, and Mac reared wildly in surprise, frightening her even more than Blade did.

"Quit fighting, girl, or this horse will bolt, and it'll be the end of us all."

The will to fight left her, her fear of the uncontrollable horse subduing her. Besides, she was too exhausted and breathless to resist the fierce strength of the man whose arms bound her so tightly against himself. As Mac galloped into the darkening twilight, away from the house, across the rough acreage of cactus and brush and oak, away from every trace of civilization to the most remote part of the ranch, the man and the woman grew aware of the erotic pleasures of riding the plunging steed together.

Jenny's hips were pressed closely into Blade's loins, and every thudding movement rocked them together until the slightest touch seared their bodies like a flame. Blade's hands moved over her as they rode, unfastening her blouse despite her feeble attempts to thwart him, so that it was warm bare flesh that he touched with his calloused fingers.

She felt his lips move hungrily beneath her streaming hair even as his hands caressed the swelling globes of her breasts. She knew she should struggle harder, that she should scream, but Blade's touch, coupled with her fear of the horse, had temporarily lulled her will to fight. Dimly, she knew she shouldn't let Blade have his way with her so easily, but even as she thought of fighting him, some part of her reveled in this moment that was as wildly glorious as her most passionate dreams about him, and she was weak with shame and delight.

The man and woman raced deeper and deeper into the black night, into a world that was primal and dark with danger and swirling passion.

9

When Blade finally halted the snorting Mac, Jenny saw the shadowy outlines of his hunting cabin in the dim light. Blade dismounted first and tied the reins to a low tree limb. Then he lifted Jenny from the horse, pulling her close to him so that her body slid against his all the way down, stirring his male senses until they screamed to possess her. To Jenny his action was familiar and insolent, and it awakened her to the reality of her situation.

As soon as her feet touched the ground she tried to run, but Blade pulled her into his arms and kissed her hard, his mouth forcing hers open to admit his tongue. He kissed her again and again with a fierce, savage hunger while she struggled in vain. At first his kisses were harsh and angry because she fought him, but after a while, as her resistance faltered, his mouth gentled upon hers until at last the kisses he rained upon her pouting, bruised lips were infinitely tender. Finally he dragged his

155

lips from the sweet, wanton delight of her mouth, but he went on holding her, his whole body trembling.

"Do you know what it did to me, seeing you with Mike tonight?" he admitted roughly, shaking lips pressed into her hair, in a voice that vibrated through every part of her being. "To think of you married to him? Of you lying with him in his bed? Of him owning you the way Dean did?" Blade's grip tightened on her slim shoulders from the torture his thoughts aroused. "For months I've wanted you, Jenny. I can't bear the thought of losing you to him the way I lost you to Dean. Just as I don't think I can live if you don't let me have you tonight."

"Why are you giving me a choice now?" Her voice was light and breathless. "I thought you were carrying me off to—"

"Rape you," he finished. There was bitter shame in his low words.

"Yes."

She could feel the violent pounding of his heart beneath her ear.

"I've never yet taken a woman who didn't come to me willingly. I guess tonight is as close as I've ever come. But you can go back to the house, Jenny, if you want to. I won't stop you."

He held her locked against his hard thighs, and she sensed what his agony would be if she demanded that he release her. He was giving her back the thing she had fought for so desperately when she'd run from him in the woods—her freedom of choice. She had only to say, "Take me back," and he would. But for some strange reason she said nothing, even though to delay only added to her danger. At any moment he might lose control again and change his mind.

She stared up at him in silence, tormented by the

chaos of her emotions just as he was tormented by his. She wanted him even though she thought the wanting was wrong without commitment. Now that he was being serious, he'd made no mention of marriage, only of passion. But she was not made for the easy kind of loving Blade accepted as the normal pattern between a man and a woman.

Gently, Blade bent his gold head to hers again, and his hands spanned her tiny waist. He seemed so big and so magnificently powerful against her smaller, feminine body. He was so virile. Everything about him thrilled her, his hands on her waist, his lips in her hair, his throbbing, barely leashed male passion.

"Jenny girl," he began softly, caressingly. "These past few months have been a living hell for me. I know I've never been half good enough to deserve a woman like you, but I've always wanted you. I couldn't stand you thinking of me the way everyone in town always has, feeling that I'm no good, that any intimacy with me would be like wallowing in filth, that my touch would taint you."

"I never thought that, Blade," she said quietly.

"You said it, that day at the corral."

"That was because you'd made me mad by goading me about Mike, and by saying you were going to date another woman. I was jealous and hurt."

"I haven't looked at another woman since I moved back to the ranch, Jenny."

"But what about Susan Harper?" Jenny blurted out.

"Susan again? Girl, when are you going to give up on that? I don't care about her. What makes you think I do?"

"Blade, I—"

Blade heard the trembling hurt in her voice. "Jenny, Susan has never been important to me, and I don't matter to her, either. Didn't you yourself say she was back with her ex-husband?"

Jenny hovered on the verge of admitting she'd seen Susan in his room, but what was the use? Obviously that had meant nothing more to Blade than the satisfaction of a passing need. Sadly, Jenny realized that he probably saw his desire for her in the same light, and she hesitated.

"Blade, I don't know what to do. We're so different, you and I. We don't think alike about a lot of very important things. We don't share the same values."

"Yes, I suppose we are different in a lot of ways, but I value *you*, Jenny. Maybe that's more important than anything else between a man and a woman."

Could he value her for anything more than her body? she wondered, and her heart ached with the fear that he couldn't.

His voice went on in the soft darkness. "I've told myself it was crazy, my wanting you when I wasn't the kind of man you wanted or deserved. I tried to put you out of my mind, to think of the resort, to think of anything, Jenny, except you. Still, there were times I thought I wouldn't be able to stop myself from coming to your room and forcing you to give me what I wanted because I needed you so much. That made me feel low, as if I were no better than an animal, with no control. I couldn't stand watching you at the resort, so I tried to avoid you. But you were always around, so serene, so untouched, so unreachable. Girl, you drive me crazy, you're so beautiful. So I went on wanting you, dreaming of taking you. Sometimes I thought that if I did force you, I could make you accept me and forget Mike and Dean and whoever else might be in your thoughts. But I can't force you, Jenny. I don't ever want to hurt you. I'm sorry

I scared you tonight, chasing you. There was a demon riding me when I saw you like that with Mike.''

Something inside Jenny surrendered, and she knew with sudden, painful insight that she loved Blade, that she had always loved him. That she had always been afraid of loving him. She'd even married his brother because she was so afraid of her feelings. It was not anything bad within Blade that she'd feared; rather, it was his power to unleash a heart that she'd bound so tightly with her prudishness and hypocrisy. She was afraid of real love, of the giving up to another of herself, of the terrible risk involved. And now, even though she was more afraid than ever, she knew that if she didn't risk everything for this man, even the values of a lifetime, she risked her very life itself. Maybe she and Blade didn't want the same things or see life from the same slant. Maybe she couldn't bind him with the conventional ropes of marriage and eternal fidelity, but she would never know what they could share together if she didn't take a chance and meet him halfway.

In that blinding instant she decided to give herself to Blade on his terms, to demand nothing from him in return, no matter what the inevitable cost to herself.

"There's no one in my thoughts except you, Blade Taylor,'' she admitted shyly, tears of happiness and love shining in her eyes. "And you've already ruined my reputation now, haven't you? Maybe it's high time I earned my black name.''

He smiled at her as he read her meaning, a slow, crookedly charming smile that brightened her heart, and then he placed a large hand on either side of her face and kissed her long and deeply and very tenderly.

She broke away and murmured, "I'm beginning to

think there's some truth in what you said this afternoon. There may be great pleasure in living up to my wicked reputation."

"Wanton!" he murmured in that silky voice of his that could make shivers trace through her. He laughed as he lifted her into his arms. "There'll be great pleasure, my love. I promise you."

He lifted her into his arms and carried her into the cabin, laying her upon the bed and following her down.

"Jenny, my darling Jenny."

Months of frustration and pain spilled out of him as his lips lowered to hers in a light, undemanding kiss that belied the intensity of his desire, a gentle kiss that made her moan softly, longing for him to deepen it. But he was determined to take her slowly, to arouse her fully before he assuaged his own all-consuming need.

With expert ease he undressed her, unbuttoning her blouse with fingers that brushed her bare flesh, unfastening her jeans, sliding the garments from her creamy skin until she lay gleaming and naked in the streaming moonlight. She was as beautiful as she'd been in his dreams, green eyes passionately afire. It seemed to him that he'd wanted her for all eternity.

He stripped, shedding his boots first with a clatter upon the plank floor and then his shirt. He was bronzed and naked when he came to her and wrapped his arms around her again, positioning her beneath him, their bodies molten everywhere they touched, flesh upon flesh, man upon woman. He groaned with pleasure at the rounded softness of her belly and the long smoothness of her legs against his hard, muscled length.

"Open your mouth to me," he said huskily. "I want to taste you."

She let his tongue slide inside, and he kissed her

deeply, intimately, savoring the wet, sweet warmth of her.

His mouth glided down the pale column of her throat, kissing her beneath her ears, along the delicate line of her jaw, hesitating at the base of her throat, his lips lingering upon her madly beating pulse. Then his golden head moved lower and she felt his teeth and tongue gently playing across her nipples.

Her fingers wound into the thick, bright fall of his hair, and she brought his face back to hers so that he kissed her again on the mouth. His fierce kisses enflamed her, and she sighed, clinging to him, aching for him.

But he went on caressing her and kissing her until she thought she would burst with desire. At last she felt his hand move between her legs, and he touched her, the gentle, stroking motion of his fingers sliding over her, manipulating soft flesh into heated arousal, his fingertips teasing at first, and then evoking exquisite quivers of sensation that built until she thought she would die if he didn't take her.

She arched her body against his, moving her hips against the thrilling pleasure of his hand, but it was not his hand that she wanted.

"Love me, Blade . . . I can't stand it anymore if you don't. Quickly. Please. Oh . . . quickly."

Her passionate demand, whispered hotly against his ear, excited him more than anything, and he took his hand away and swept her beneath him, fitting her body to his, entering her carefully and moving slowly and rhythmically at first, until his passion consumed him and he could hold back no longer, he could only give vent to the raging force that drove him. Her body was splendor, sweet, savage, shattering splendor that drew him out of himself until he shuddered deep within her. Only vaguely was he aware of the way she clung to him desperately, her fulfillment a tremor that seemed to go on and on even after his own body stopped shaking.

Afterward, he did not release her, but went on holding her, her head cradled in the crook of his arm, her hair spilling in silken waves upon the pillow. One of her hands lay upon his stomach, the other lightly caressed his jaw. Their faces were so close that she felt his warm breath stir against her skin as he stared deeply, lovingly into her eyes. She felt that she belonged to him utterly, even if he could never belong utterly to her.

Despite her doubts about the future and about Blade's ability to love her as deeply as she loved him, Jenny had never been more blissfully happy. She'd never known the passion of this night in ten years of marriage, yet for once she was able to think of Dean without guilt. He belonged to the past, and she'd been as good a wife to him as she could be. Now she loved Blade.

She knew Blade lacked Dean's faithful nature, but perhaps it was selfish to ask for lasting love when Blade could satisfy her so gloriously, so completely. For the moment what they had together made all other needs seem trivial.

"I love you, Jenny," he murmured in a strange, broken voice.

She didn't know that he'd never said those words to a woman before, and though she was thrilled, she wondered what he really meant by them. Did he say that to every woman who pleased him in bed? That thought brought her both pain and pleasure, pain to think of other women sleeping with Blade, pleasure because she knew she had made him physically happy.

His hand drifted over her body, across her breasts to her stomach. "You could have a child," he said, "if we aren't more careful. I wanted you so much, I didn't think. I'm sorry, Jenny."

His words unwittingly brought more pain because they reminded her that he was not the kind of man who would make such a commitment to a woman. She wanted his child. She wanted *him*. She wanted marriage and a lifetime together, while he wanted none of those things. Was life really so simple for him? she wondered. She supposed that it was.

A sweet, aching sadness engulfed her, making her feel lost and afraid, and she pressed her face into his chest for comfort as she began to cry for all the things she wanted and could never share with him. Blade's arms tightened around her, her tears wracking him with torture and guilt. She had cried that first time so long ago, and two days later she'd married Dean. What had he done to make her cry, when all he wanted was to make her happy? Blade wondered.

"Don't cry, Jenny. I can't stand it when you cry."

He searched and found her lips and kissed her with all the passion in his being, and she returned his kisses, seeking the numbing comfort his lovemaking could give her, enflaming him again with her fierce caresses and the provocative movement of her body rubbing against his, until once more desire seared them and swept them in its burning tide.

In the splendor of his loving she forgot, but only for the moment, all that she could never have.

Six weeks passed, six sensual weeks of passion and the questing for fulfillment. During the days when Blade and Jenny worked at the resort, when each knew the other was near but they couldn't be together, a fever burned in both of them. Neither could wait for the evenings when they could be alone, those hours after Maria put Cathy to sleep and went to bed herself. Then Jenny would slip out of the house and go to Blade's room. He would be waiting for her, as eager and filled with desire as she. She would run to him, and they would melt into one another's arms, clinging, kissing, seeking the glory that only one could give the other.

Sometimes he would draw her down on the bed, covering her breasts with his hands, softly massaging her, sliding his hands over her body even before he undressed her. Sometimes when they were naked he lay back and pulled her down on top of him, easing her body onto his, encouraging her to make love to him. Straddling him, she would move slowly at first, watching his face, exulting in the passion she aroused in him. His fingers would trace lightly back and forth along her spine or move up across her belly to cup her breasts.

Blade was a passionate man, and he made love to her with a completeness she had never known before. For Blade, touching Jenny and being with her was his heaven upon earth. She was the mate of his soul, and his physical love for her was sacred. Sometimes he was wild, sometimes gentle, but every time they were together he made her feel she was the only woman on earth who could arouse him thus. He made her feel infinitely precious. Her love deepened, and she fell more and more under his spell, until it seemed to Jenny that there was no part of her that did not belong to Blade.

He had no inhibitions, and with him she shed the modesty of a lifetime as he taught her the wonders of love. He pleasured her with his lips and tongue, overriding her initial protests, encouraging her to make love to him in the same way, until soon she found she gloried in this kind of loving as much as he. Sometimes they rode their horses far out over the ranch, and he would find some beautiful, deserted bower for their love. Once, when they were hot and dirty from a long ride, he playfully pulled her into the creek fully dressed. The sight of her blouse clinging to her thrusting breasts made him forget his playfulness, and he made love to her in the middle of that scorching spring day as they stood there together, wet mouths fused. He held her closely, plunging deep within her body, while the cool green waters of the creek curled around their legs. Afterward they swam and laughed and made love again.

Blade awakened fully the earthy sensuality in her nature that she had struggled so long to suppress, and Jenny lived those weeks in a daze of happiness. It was only when she was not with him that she doubted his love.

One night, after they'd made love, she asked him about the scars crisscrossing his lower back and thighs.

He frowned, and she felt a sudden, inexplicable tension in his body before he rolled from her and crossed his arms over his chest. For a while he stared in silence at the ceiling, and she didn't know if he was going to answer her. He looked so bleak. When he finally spoke, his voice was so low she could scarcely hear him, the sound seeming to be dragged out of him.

"I was wounded in Lebanon."

Tentatively, she reached out and touched the ridged flesh on his legs, and he winced at her light touch.

"How?" she whispered.

"It's not something I've ever been able to talk about—with anyone."

"Please tell me. Maybe it would make it easier for you if you shared it."

"I don't want to burden you with my pain, Jenny."

She saw an anguish in his eyes that was past her comprehension. "But I want to know."

"No, you don't. Not really," he replied quietly. "You only say that because you don't understand." For an instant his expression softened. "How can anyone understand the insanity of war? You just live through it if you have to."

"It's over," she said gently.

"For me, maybe. For those left—" He shuddered. "It was hell over there, like I've never been through before or since. I guess it still is."

Jenny could feel him trembling, and she caressed him, seeking to comfort him.

"Just tell me a part of it, Blade."

He attempted to, in a remote voice that didn't sound at all like his own. "I tried to save an Arab kid who had been hit by shrapnel, but he died in my arms." He stopped. For a moment he was too shaken to go on. "Maybe it was better that he did, poor kid, because he was cut to shreds. I was shot trying to rescue him. Damn it, Jenny, he died because of what we did—maybe even because of me."

"Not because of you, Blade. Never because of you."

A cold sweat broke out on Blade's forehead as he relived that day. He remembered it all, the ceaseless, ear-shattering explosions, the stench of burning oil, the black curls of smoke above orange flames, the heat, the perpetual buzz of flies, the choking dust in the streets every time a jeep or tank zoomed past. The child had been hit in the street, and Blade had braved enemy crossfire in his vain attempt to save him. He'd scooped the child from the rubble, cradling that helpless bundle in his arms as he ran for cover. Three bullets had ripped into Blade just a second before he reached safety. In searing pain, he'd had to crawl the last few feet to reach the American lines. He'd handed the child to a soldier and then pitched forward into the dirt and his own blood. Mercifully, he hadn't regained consciousness for two days. He'd almost died, and he'd been given a medal for that act of heroism, though he never spoke of it. He couldn't speak of it now, not even to Jenny. The horror of combat was something that was locked deep inside him.

"I can't talk about it. Don't ask me any more."

Blade's blue eyes were stark and empty. He never voluntarily brought up his time in the Marines, and after his attempt to answer he lapsed into silence, trying to put the hellish images out of his mind. He wanted only to protect Jenny from the terror and hell he'd experienced.

But Jenny wanted to draw him out. She knew that his life had not been smooth and protected, as hers had been. If they were ever to understand each other she realized she was going to have to force him to reveal himself.

"This scar on your leg looks different from the others," she persisted, indicating a jagged line on his tanned thigh. "It's not so raw and new-looking."

Her hand traced the length of wrinkled skin. He'd never told anyone the truth about that scar, but that memory was the bitterest of all. Strangely, he could speak of it now, though. It seemed almost as if it had happened in another lifetime.

His voice was dry and hard when he spoke. "That's where my father, not Caleb, but Jamie, laid me open with his screwdriver when he was drunk and I jumped between him and my mother—before she ran away and left us. He was crazy that night. He would have sliced me to ribbons if I hadn't run off and stayed away for three days.

I was eight years old. He worked my mother over real good that night."

He stopped, gripped with tension. Now she would recoil and think him little better than an animal. What did a gentle woman like Jenny know of the sordid ugliness of life or the hellish bloodline that flowed in his veins?

"Oh, Blade, Blade, how terrible it all must have been for you." Her fingers were lightly caressing his scar as if to comfort him. "Where did you go when you ran away?" Her heart went out to that poor lost child.

"Caleb found me sleeping under a bridge, half frozen, and he took me in until my old man came after me."

Jenny was too horrified to speak; she lay in rigid silence as she pondered the pain of his childhood. At last she said, "I don't think I've ever appreciated my own childhood until right now. My family was strict, but loving. They never deliberately hurt one another. I still miss both my parents. You probably don't remember, but you wrote me a letter when they died in that car wreck not long after Caleb's death. It meant a lot to me, Blade, your writing when I felt so awful about them."

"I wrote because you were always special to me, even back then, Jenny," he said softly, pushing a strand of hair back over her ear. That was as close as he could come to admitting the depth of his love for her; he was still afraid that in the end she would reject him. Blade had been based in Japan when he'd heard about her parents. He'd known she was hurting, and he'd wanted to be with her to share her pain, but he couldn't get leave. How he'd envied Dean. Blade had thought of Jenny constantly, knowing she was going through a difficult period. "It wasn't enough, my writing. I should have come home."

"Dean was there," she said quietly. "I guess there wasn't much anyone could have done."

"Yes," he said, frowning, her mention of Dean reminding him that she'd had no need of him as long as Dean had been alive. Blade wished with all his heart that he was more like Dean or Kilpatrick; this conversation about their backgrounds had made him realize again how different Jenny and he really were. Could a woman like her ever be happy with a man like him?

Because he couldn't say the things he wanted to, he pulled her into his arms and showed her, in the only way he knew how, how much he loved her. Within moments her mood was as passionate as his, and she was breathless and throbbing with desire when he pulled away.

"Blade, w-why are you stopping?"

He smiled at her eagerness as he gathered her once more into his arms and bent his brow to hers with affectionate playfulness so that they touched, brow to brow, nose to nose. "The other night, didn't you admit that you'd wanted to make love in the hayloft the day I kissed you in the corral?"

She nodded, and her eyes were sparkling as he lifted her effortlessly and strode toward the door. "Blade, don't you think we should take a quilt?"

He set her down. "And I thought you were too breathless and passionate for such practical considerations."

"Forget the quilt then," she said.

"Not on your life." He picked up a blanket and took her hand in his, leading her out the door. "I want to indulge your fantasy, girl, not cope with scratches from that prickly hay for the next year."

They ran toward the barn, laughing in the moonlight like children. When at last they reached the loft and spread the blanket down upon a bed of hay, Blade stood very still and held out his hand. She went eagerly into his arms, abandoning herself to the physical pleasure of his lips and tongue and thrusting male body until he made her his in a searing blaze of passion that left them dazed anew with the wonder of their love.

After that, there was a new, unspoken closeness between them. Blade spent time with Cathy and seemed to enjoy the antics of the two-year-old. He even tried to convince Cathy to give up her thumb, but he got no farther than Jenny had, and Jenny teased him unmercifully about his failure. It wasn't that Cathy didn't take great interest in his attempts to make her stop sucking her thumb, because she did. She would run to him and say, with a dimple and a giggle, holding a bottle of thumb-paint proudly, "Paint, Uncle Blade. Paint Cathy's thumb."

He would laugh and then try to be stern. "Okay, I'll paint it, you little rascal, but that means you're not supposed to suck it after I do. And I don't want to hear you sneaking into the bathroom and washing it off like you did yesterday. You're a big girl now. Big girls don't suck their thumbs."

Cathy would only nod brightly while he painted both thumbs. "Some big girls do, Uncle Blade."

He would laugh as he talked to her, and Jenny would laugh at them both. It was never long before Cathy found some pretext to wash her hands, and her thumb would be back in her mouth as usual.

"Hell, Jenny, she even sucks her thumb when she's asleep. Didn't you say you bought a book on this subject? I think it's time one of us read it."

"Maybe it's time you listened to me for a change, darling. She'll give up her thumb when she's ready."

"You know, that advice is sounding more sensible

every time I hear it. I wonder why I didn't think of it myself."

Jenny would have been very happy if she thought Blade truly loved her as she loved him, but the more deeply she fell in love with him, the more terrible it seemed to her that he couldn't love a woman with his heart and soul, that he didn't want to make the commitment of marriage. Jenny was increasingly aware of the town's growing speculation about them as a couple; though Blade now took great care to be discreet, one look at Jenny's radiant face when her eyes met his told all. And no matter how often she told herself that giving up her virtuous reputation was worth it if she could lie in Blade's arms at night, she was bothered by having an affair with him.

Jenny lay awake many nights, unable to sleep, because deep in her heart she felt it was wrong to sleep with Blade if she wasn't married to him, no matter how beautiful their relationship was. But she said nothing to Blade; she didn't want to push him into a commitment he was uncomfortable making. After his one mention of marriage in front of Mike, Blade had never again brought up the subject.

June came, and with it the blasting, dry heat of a Texas hill country summer. Air conditioners hummed full-time. Guests loitered in the shade and swam in the pool and creek for relief. Jenny consumed huge quantities of iced tea and cold water. Outside, in the middle of the day, the ranch seemed as hot as a furnace. Despite the heat, the resort overflowed with guests, though not as many as Blade said they needed, but the more guests, the more Blade worked.

Despite the depressed state of the Texas hotel business

in general, Blade was working terribly hard to make the resort a success. Sometimes he would call Jenny into his office to go over the statistics they were up against.

"Jenny, do you realize that in Houston hotels the occupancy rate averages less than fifty percent—and many of those rooms are filled by discounting, sometimes drastically? Their business still hasn't recovered from all the overbuilding in the industry, the devaluation of the Mexican peso, and the stagnation of the oil business."

"But we're not competing with Houston."

"I'm afraid we are. We can't raise our rates because we have to be able to offer a comparable package to conventions. Woodlands Hideaway doesn't have a location that's as easily accessible as Houston, Dallas, or San Antonio, so we've got to fight them for every nickel of business."

Blade began to travel. He had brochures printed. He made contacts with travel agents, promoting Woodlands Hideaway with zeal and determination, but secretly, Jenny wondered if he traveled because he was growing restless. When he was in Zachery Falls he was with her constantly. But more and more he was on the road, and Jenny was afraid that when he was gone he sought the company of other women. Even though he called her every night while he was gone, she couldn't bring herself to fully trust him; she was too unsure of herself as a woman. She didn't know it, but Blade understood her feelings. For all his outward toughness, he was gentle and sensitive toward her, never deliberately inflicting hurt, but this only made her believe more strongly than ever that he was simply showing her consideration by not chasing women in Zachery Falls.

When she was besieged with doubts, she would remember that she'd never been wild and fun-loving like the Susan Harpers of the world. Was it any surprise that a man like Blade, who was not inexperienced with women, would want variety? How could he be satisfied with her?

She made herself miserable when he was gone, but she never told him of her jealousy for fear that would drive him even farther away. Blade sensed that something was wrong, but she denied it when he asked her, though her silence afterward made him worry even more. He thought that he regretted their relationship, and, as always, he believed that he was not good enough for her, that he should go away and leave her so she could marry a man more her type, like Mike Kilpatrick. He remembered how she'd married Dean ten years ago, and he wondered if she wouldn't be engaged to Kilpatrick now if he hadn't returned and practically forced himself upon her.

So they went on, Blade and Jenny, loving each other yet not understanding the secret unhappinesses locked in one another's hearts.

10

Pregnant! The word had thrummed in Jenny's brain during the hour-long drive from her doctor's office in Austin back to Zachery Falls.

For once Jenny was glad that Blade was out of town on business. She was so upset that she could never have concealed her distress from him.

Standing before the full-length mirror in her bedroom, Jenny slowly took off her clothes, shedding the garments one by one into a heap on the floor. She stared at her nude body, running her hands across her smooth belly. Already her breasts were fuller, her complexion more glowing.

A mixture of wonder, pride, and shame filled her—she was carrying Blade's child. Since that first night, he had taken every precaution to avoid pregnancy. Though he'd never mentioned his reasons, she guessed that a child was the last thing he wanted, and the prospect of telling him that she had conceived sent a shiver of doubt through her. Nonetheless, a part of her was ecstatic. She loved Blade, and she wanted his child.

But the next moment she remembered the difficulty of her situation, and her joy faded. She wasn't married. Blade had never even hinted at that possibility. How could she go on living in Zachery Falls? People would talk. It wouldn't be fair to the baby, nor to Cathy. For the first time Jenny was almost glad that her strict mother and father were not alive; they would be spared this shame.

Jenny sank down on the bed and huddled beneath a blanket, feeling mortified and frightened at the thought of being an unwed mother at this stage of her life. What on earth was she going to do? What would Blade say if she told him? Would he think she was trying to trap him into marriage? Everyone had always said that he wasn't the marrying kind. She didn't want to make him unhappy, but the child was his. She had to tell him. What if he rejected her and the baby? The mere thought brought a crushing sensation of sorrow and the first sting of tears to her eyes. She closed her eyelids tightly so they wouldn't spill. She was afraid that if she let herself cry, she would never stop. Oh, what, what was she going to do?

She'd been heedlessly reckless, selfish and unthinking in her love for Blade. Why hadn't she thought of how this might affect Cathy? But she had. Blade had been careful never to sleep with her in the house. She'd always left him and returned to her own bed, so that Maria would not know that she had slept with him. He never touched her in public.

Oh, why had this happened when they'd been so careful every time but that first night? Pregnancy couldn't possibly be hidden for long, and Jenny knew that her condition would force all the secrets of her heart into the open. She and her baby would be a matter of common, unkind gossip very shortly if she didn't take steps to prevent it.

There was only one thing she could do. She would have to leave for a while, perhaps forever, but first she had to tell Blade.

Blade returned from his business trip that evening, and he was so happy about the three conventions he had booked for the slow winter season that she couldn't bring herself to tell him her news that first night. It was too heavenly to slip into his arms and let him make love to her, to pretend that everything was just the same between them. A week stole past, and then another. Jenny was so afraid that her news would drive Blade away that every hour that she did not tell him seemed to her an hour that she still had him. The thought of telling him became more and more difficult to face. Because she hadn't told him that first night, not telling him now became the easiest course.

Blade was aware that something was wrong, and he was terribly afraid that Jenny was trying to work up the nerve to tell him that it was over between them. So he didn't press her whenever she seemed to be on the verge of confiding in him. Instead, he would shush her and hold her and kiss her until the flame of passion consumed them and there could be no thought of anything other than letting the wildness of their need wash over them.

One hot afternoon when they were out riding Jenny was overcome by nausea. Usually she enjoyed their late-evening rides, but that day they had decided to ride earlier than usual. The heat was stifling; no breeze stirred the leaves or high grasses. Jenny had forgotten her wide-brimmed hat, and the sun baked down upon her. Trickles of sweat ran down her back beneath her cotton blouse as she fought to suppress her queasiness, but her sickness would not be restrained.

"Blade, please, help me down," she cried weakly, her embarrassment and fear nearly as acute as her nausea as her gaze met his.

He dismounted and was beside her in an instant, his tanned face grave with concern.

"What's the matter? Jenny, you look ill. Darling, why didn't you tell me—"

"I—"

Jenny took a deep breath in an attempt to control her mounting sickness as he lifted her from the mare. When her feet touched the ground, she pushed against his arms and ran a little distance away, turning her back to him.

"Don't look!" she gasped. "Please. Don't." Then she bent over, unable to say more.

The spasm was long and painful, but at last, when she was able to lift her head and breathe in the fresh air without feeling ill, she became aware of Blade's critical gaze. She still felt weak and shaky, but the nausea had subsided.

"The sun was so hot," she stammered. "I'm sorry."

His blue eyes were piercing. "Riding doesn't usually make you sick."

"Blade—"

"You're pregnant, aren't you?"

She stared at him bleakly, hopelessly.

"Yes."

"Why didn't you tell me?"

"Because—" His dark look choked off all utterance. It was obvious he wasn't happy about the baby at all. "Blade, I never meant for this to happen."

His expression grew even darker, but his eyes were more brilliant than ever. "And obviously you're none too pleased."

"Blade, that's not how I feel. You don't understand."

"Oh, I understand, but you're much too kind to tell me the truth. I've known something was bothering you for a long time, Jenny." He paused, his expression softening as he regarded her white, troubled face and reminded himself that she was unwell and carrying his child. "But this is hardly the time or place for this discussion. I want to get you out of the sun and back to the house. If I'd known you were pregnant I would never have asked you to ride and risk harming you or the baby."

He led her back to the mare and helped her to mount, but he did not climb back on Mac. Instead he walked, leading both horses slowly, asking Jenny often if she was all right.

Jenny was fine now except for the knot of fear that bound her emotions. Blade was grimly silent between his concerned questions regarding her health, and his silence frightened her.

When they reached the house, Blade helped her down and led the horses to the corral without a word. She watched him go, filled with a black, devastating sorrow at the thought of losing him. She wanted to weep and scream and run after him to beg him not to leave her, but pride stiffened her back and saved her from that last humiliation. Feeling drained, she turned and went slowly into the house.

Blade felt like a man who was dying inside. He loved her, but he knew she could never love him. What woman could—the way he'd been raised? The way he'd lived. He'd tried to change, to live the past down. He'd gone to college and then joined the Marines. He thought of the long years of work and sacrifice. Was it all for nothing? It seemed so now. He didn't know how to make Jenny love him; what could he do that he hadn't already done? Jenny only wanted him, in the way he'd wanted all the other women he'd ever known besides her. He understood that kind of wanting well enough, the fire of physical attraction, the fleeting satiation of a sensual need that never touched the soul. Blade was sure Jenny was still ashamed of her feelings for him.

He remembered how she'd loved Dean, how she'd chosen him all those years ago, even after she and Blade had made love. Blade had known then that he loved her, but what woman wouldn't have taken Dean over himself when the whole town believed he was rotten, no matter what he did? What did Blade Taylor know about gentleness and faithfulness, they were saying even now, about being a husband to a woman like Jenny Zachery? Blade knew better than Jenny what was being said behind their backs. He knew that people pitied her, believing that beneath his polished surface he was as bad as ever, that he'd only come back to take her money and to cheat her out of what was rightfully hers, that he was temporarily putting on a damn good act. They were saying that Blade Taylor had always broken the heart of any woman he'd ever gotten close to, and Jenny Zachery would be no different. He'd take her for everything she had and then leave her without even her pride. In that moment, Blade hated himself almost as much as he hated the world.

Blade unsaddled Red and then mounted Mac again. He had to go off and be by himself for a while. Maybe it was time he left Zachery Falls for good. Maybe that was what was best for Jenny in the long run. Maybe a kid was better off not knowing his father if his father was Blade Taylor.

Blade swung himself easily into the saddle. Digging in his heels, he galloped away, past the house, past the window Jenny stood before. He was too filled with pain to even glance her way. Jenny watched him, and her sadness was even greater than his because she had the terrible feeling that he'd left her forever.

Somehow Jenny lived through that long, hot, sultry afternoon in a daze of misery. Everyone had warned her, hadn't they, and now there was no one she could turn to for comfort. She was utterly alone.

"Bad blood will out," the townpeople had always said. Jenny remembered well every evil rumor she'd ever heard about Blade. Could he really be so heartless? Could he abandon her and his child without a backward glance? She remembered the way he'd kissed Susan that night in his room. Were sex and love meaningless to a man like him? Had Blade ever really belonged to her? She'd behaved foolishly, falling in love with a man like him, and now she was only paying the price.

The sun was sinking in a burst of scarlet and gold when Jenny, not wishing to face even Maria and Cathy, decided to walk down by the creek and dangle her feet in the cool water. She had the feeling that she would never see Blade again, so when she whirled at the sound of a snapping twig, it was with surprise that she met the bold blue of his eyes. Blade's expression was fierce and untamed and somehow terrifying, but his voice was oddly gentle.

"Jenny—"

Her eyes misted and she looked away. She didn't want his pity, nor his contempt.

"Blade, you didn't have to come back. You don't owe me anything."

His voice was low and tortured. "I didn't come back because I owed you anything, girl. I was going to run away the way I always ran away every time Jamie beat me when I was a kid, the way I ran away all those years ago after you married Dean. For months I've known I should have left you alone so you could have Kilpatrick. He could have run the resort, maybe better than I can. But the baby changes all that, doesn't it?" he said bitterly. "I've ruined things for you. Kilpatrick would never marry you, now that you're pregnant with Blade Taylor's child. Besides, I couldn't bear it if you married him anyway."

She turned, frowning in puzzlement. What was he saying? What did he mean? He'd said he was planning to leave. Why had he come back then?

"I know I'm the last man in the world for a woman like you. You said that once, didn't you, that if I were the last man in the world you wouldn't marry me?"

Had he actually taken seriously that remark she'd hurled at him in anger?

"Blade—"

"I want to marry you, Jenny, and before you say no—"

"Blade, just because I'm pregnant, that doesn't mean you have to marry me." Her lashes descended over her shimmering eyes. Her heart was breaking, and she was afraid she would cry.

"I know you could never love me the way you loved Dean, but I would be good to you and Cathy and the baby, Jenny. At least I would try. I've always loved this ranch. I feel like it's my home, just as it is yours. Even if you don't love me now, you're attracted to me, and we've proven we can work well together on a day-to-day basis. That's more than a lot of couples have. We'd have the child, of course, and Cathy. And as I see it, if you don't marry me, you'll be in one hell of a mess. I've cost you Kilpatrick, and you need a man to help you with the ranch and the resort. It's too much for you to deal with alone. Besides, you know how people would talk if you didn't marry. I don't want my kid growing up feeling as though he's not as good as the next kid because his real father ran off and left him. I know the pain of that too well to inflict it on my own child."

"But, Blade, it's not a question of my not loving you or not wanting to marry you. *You* don't love *me*. I don't want to force you."

"Don't love you?" He stared at her incredulously. "Don't love you! Are you crazy, girl?" He pulled her into his arms and buried his face in her long, sweet-smelling hair, his fingers digging into her slim shoulders. "I love everything about you. I've always loved you. That's why Dean and I could never get along. I always resented him because he had you. Why do you think I left here? Because I loved you and couldn't stay in Zachery Falls with you married to Dean."

"Blade," Jenny sighed tremulously, all of her pain leaving her at his admission. "Is what you're saying really true? Do you really love me?"

"There's never been anyone but you," he said.

"But you chased all those women."

"Most of that gossip was exaggerated. If I'd had half the women they said I've had, I'd be dead from exhaustion. I chased a few, I guess, but that was only because I couldn't have the one I really wanted." His lips moved in her hair. "Believe me, Jenny, I've never been the man they say I am."

"Blade, I saw you making love to Susan that night

after the hayride," she said hesitantly. "That made me think sex didn't mean much to you."

"What?"

"And I've been torturing myself thinking you must be seeing other women when you travel, that you're bored with me."

"I found Susan waiting in my room that night. I'm sorry for that, Jenny, but nothing went on. I shouldn't even have kissed her, but it happened so fast I couldn't avoid it. I never dreamed you saw us. If I'd known, I would have explained to you long before now. I told her that night that she and I could never be anything more than friends. I wanted you that night, not Susan."

"I'd be mighty gullible to fall for a fool story like that, Blade," she said with a smile. "Susan's awfully beautiful, and you were very angry with me."

"Real beauty comes from inside a woman, Jenny. You've always been the most beautiful woman in the world to me. I was mad at you, but not so mad I lost sight of the fact that it wasn't Susan I wanted and that if I took her, I was being unfair to everyone. As for the traveling, Jenny, I've been working. Don't you know yet that *you're* my woman? I don't need anyone but you if I know you're waiting for me. I don't want anyone else."

In that moment Jenny believed him, and she felt aglow with happiness. Blade Taylor loved her—imagine that! He'd always loved her, even when she'd been married to Dean. Deep in her heart she knew that she'd always loved him, too; she just hadn't realized it. Her love for Blade had been the root of her dissatisfaction in her marriage, and no wonder. Poor Dean. If only she'd seen the truth, he could have married someone who was wild about him.

"I've always been scared of loving you, Jenny, of the way it could rip me apart because I couldn't have you. I'm still scared."

"Blade, my darling, I'm just as scared, because I love you, maybe even more than you love me."

He stared at her in amazement, not really believing her. "Don't say it, Jenny, if you don't mean it."

"But I do mean it. I love you."

His arms tightened around her, and they clung to one another as though to a lifeline.

"Jenny girl," he said very tenderly. His lips sought hers in an ever-deepening kiss. At last he released her. "I can't believe you really love me. A woman like you. Who would believe it? Wild Blade Taylor marrying the preacher's daughter. Saint and sinner. You know—" his blue eyes were twinkling "—I'm almost looking forward to all the gossip our marriage is going to cause. For once I won't mind what they say, my love."

"I love you, no matter what anyone says, and I think I have for years," she whispered against his lips. "It was one of those things I locked away inside myself and tried not to think about. But ever since you came back I've wanted you unbearably. You're so strong and kind. You've worked so hard to help me. You're so handsome." She smiled shyly as she traced her fingers along the skin beneath his throat. "I love it when you touch me, when you make love to me."

"And speaking of that," he began hoarsely, his hand sliding over her body in sudden, urgent need. "You know what holding you always does to me? You stir me, girl, without even trying."

"Yes?" She smiled coyly.

"Don't tease me, Jenny," he groaned.

"That was never my intention, love," she murmured,

unbuttoning his shirt and burrowing her face against the hard muscles of his chest.

"I thought you were ashamed of having an affair with me," he said, "because you thought I wasn't good enough for you."

"In a way, I was ashamed, not because of that, but because I loved you. I didn't feel right about sleeping with you without marriage. I wanted a future with you, and children. I was afraid you didn't want those things."

"Not want those things, with you?" He stared at her in wonder. "That's all I've ever wanted, to be married to you, to have a real family, to be the father of your children. What else is there in life?"

"Oh, Blade, I'm so happy. I've never been so happy."

"Neither have I, my love."

The look in his eyes sent shivers through her. His own pulse thudded with violent desire as he swept her into his arms and carried her to a place where the grasses were soft and lush and the creek gurgled and splashed beside them.

"Remember that time we made love when we were kids, Jenny?"

"How could I ever forget?"

"After that one time, I wanted you forever, girl."

He pulled her down until they both knelt on the soft earth. Their mouths touched tentatively at first, then their kiss deepened. He moved his mouth on hers, forcing her lips apart, tasting her, possessing her with his tongue.

His breathing was heavy and ragged from their love-play. Wordlessly, they removed their clothes, each watching the other shed every item of apparel until they were both naked. For a long moment they simply looked at each other, and there was a wealth of loving as their eyes met. At last he took her hand and drew her beneath him.

A fire raged in them both. Her body trembled as he kissed her tenderly; her arms went around his neck hesitantly, her fingertips brushing the soft gold hair that curled against his earlobe. His hands glided over her, stroking her breasts, cupping their new fullness, sliding lower over her velvet soft skin until she was thoroughly roused.

There was a moist ache in her most feminine place. He touched her there, arousing her with his long, lean fingers, probing, caressing, until she was as breathless as he. She was quivering, and her soft flesh felt delicious beneath his fingertips, smooth as silk and warm as melting wax.

He kissed her again upon her lush, half-open lips, his kiss as fierce and burning as his love. She was his. Truly his. Only his. No one would ever take her from him again. This realization sweetened their lovemaking for Blade and heightened his passionate need. Her hands moved over his muscled shoulders and closed tightly around his back so that she could push her body fully against his. He groaned and pressed her further into the deep grasses, exciting her with the virile loving of his masculine body.

Jenny burned with desire and sensual delight. With her arms laced around his powerful body and her legs entwined wantonly with his, she cried his name again and again, almost begging as their passion carried them to soaring, volcanic heights. Together they exploded, and waves as hotly molten as lava crashed over them as they clung to one another.

"My love, my darling, my wife," he murmured gently.

Her green eyes opened slowly and lifted to his, drowsy with languorous fulfillment and love. "Blade, I'm so happy. No man could ever make me happier. I love you."

He'd waited a lifetime to hear her say those words. As he stared down at her, he took in her voluptuous beauty. Her cheeks were flushed, her lips reddened and full. She wore the look of a sated woman very much in love.

She was his. At last. Only his.

"And I love you, only you," he said tenderly. "I always have, and I always will."

They kissed each other again, their kiss a promise that their love would last forever.

Silhouette Special Edition

SEPTEMBER TITLES

DAZZLE
Ann Major

SARAH'S CHILD
Linda Howard

STOLEN THUNDER
Natalie Bishop

INTRIGUE IN VENICE
Tracy Sinclair

A DANGEROUS PRECEDENT
Lisa Jackson

AN ACQUIRED TASTE
Kathryn Thiels

Four New
Silhouette Romances
could be yours
ABSOLUTELY FREE

Did you know that Silhouette Romances are no longer available from the shops in the U.K?

Read on to discover how you could receive four brand new Silhouette Romances, **free** and **without obligation,** with this special introductory offer to the new Silhouette Reader Service.

As thousands of women who have read these books know — Silhouette Romances sweep you away into an exciting love filled world of fascination between men and women. A world filled with

age-old conflicts — love and money, ambition and guilt, jealousy and pride, even life and death.

Silhouette Romances are the latest stories written by the world's best romance writers, and they are **only** available from Silhouette Reader Service. Take out a subscription and you could receive 6 brand new titles every month, plus a newsletter bringing you all the latest information from Silhouette's New York editors. All this delivered in one exciting parcel direct to your door, with no charges for postage and packing.

And at only 95p for a book, Silhouette Romances represent the very best value in Romantic Reading.

Remember, Silhouette Romances are **only** available to subscribers, so don't miss out on this very special opportunity. Fill in the certificate below and post it today. You don't even need a stamp.

Silhouette Desire

Your chance to write back!

We'll send you details of an exciting free offer from *SILHOUETTE*, if you can help us by answering the few simple questions below.

Just fill in this questionnaire, tear it out and put it in an envelope and post today to: Silhouette Reader Survey, FREEPOST, P.O. Box 236, Croydon, Surrey CR9 9EL. You don't even need a stamp.

What is the title of the *SILHOUETTE Desire* you have just read?

_____

How much did you enjoy it?

Very much ☐   Quite a lot ☐   Not very much ☐

Would you buy another *SILHOUETTE Desire* book?

Yes ☐   Possibly ☐   No ☐

How did you discover *SILHOUETTE Desire* books?

Advertising ☐   A friend ☐   Seeing them on sale ☐

Elsewhere (please state) _____

How often do you read romantic fiction?

Frequently ☐   Occasionally ☐   Rarely ☐

Name (Mrs/Miss) _____

Address _____

_____

_____

_____ **Postcode** _____

Age group: Under 24 ☐   25–34 ☐   35–44 ☐

45–55 ☐   Over 55 ☐

Silhouette Reader Service, P.O. Box 236, Croydon, Surrey CR9 9EL.
Readers in South Africa—write to:
Silhouette Romance Club,
Private Bag X3010, Randburg 2125.

SD1